How to
Pick Up
a Maid

IN STATUE SQUARE

How to
Pick Up
a Maid
IN STATUE SQUARE

REA TARVYDAS

thistledown press

Thistledown Press Ltd.
410 2nd Avenue North
Saskatoon, Saskatchewan, S7K 2C3
www.thistledownpress.com

Library and Archives Canada Cataloguing in Publication

Tarvydas, Rea, author
How to pick up a maid in Statue Square / Rea Tarvydas.
Short stories.
Issued in print and electronic formats.
ISBN 978-1-77187-117-4 (paperback). –ISBN 978-1-77187-118-1
(html). – ISBN 978-1-77187-119-8 (pdf)
I. Title.
PS8639.A773H69 2016   C813'.6   C2016-905256-7
C2016-905257-5

Cover and book design by Jackie Forrie
Printed and bound in Canada

Thistledown Press gratefully acknowledges the financial assistance of the Canada Council for the Arts, the Saskatchewan Arts Board, and the Government of Canada for its publishing program.

How to Pick Up a Maid

IN STATUE SQUARE

For Robert

CONTENTS

How to Pick Up a Maid
in Statue Square

Stay in Saturday night and atone for Friday's excesses: assorted amphetamines and extracurricular activities on The Filthy Acre. Calm yourself. You're coming down, simultaneously jittery and depressed. Swear off amphetamines. Think about calling home. You should stay in touch. Don't call your wife. Ex-wife.

Get up at a reasonable hour on Sunday morning; 11:00 AM is fine. Tidy the flat, empty except for the baby grand your ex-wife[1] left behind, a bed and a couple modern black leather chairs. Hide necessary electronics behind cabinets. It's more orderly that way. Remind yourself to buy a couple of abstract paintings.

Work out at the gym downstairs; you've gained weight. Shower, dress casually, and grab your messenger bag, cellphone, and a fully charged and loaded iPod. The playlist for the day

[1] You ran into her last summer when you were back home on business. She was out shopping with a man and you stared at her so you could ignore him. She looked at you as if she expected you to say something important. Instead, you imagined her lying naked across a rumpled bed and then you wondered if she liked it more with him than with you.

9

includes at least one Hunters and Collectors tune and an assortment of Manchester's finest bands, past or present. Your choice. Grab a light lunch on the way down to Central.

Filipina maids take communion on their rest day. Each Sunday at noon Central District transforms into a refugee camp. The sidewalks and pedestrian overpasses line with thousands and thousands of women. They gather in any available shade, singing, reading the Bible, gossiping and eating, fixing each other's hair, and applying makeup brought back from home. This is a sacred place.

The hollow tangle of Tagalog lures you into Statue Square, the centre of this estrogen universe. Sir Thomas Jackson, a British banker responsible for building colonial Hong Kong, presides. His eyes are empty holes. Standing, one hand grasping his black waistcoat, the other at the ready. You swear Sir Jackson's about to remove his coat, launch himself into the crowd, and body surf.

Wander through the congested square until a maid makes eye contact. Stop and chat. Flirt politely. Wonder what she'll do when she's in bed, you never know. Remember the one with the tattoo writhing above her luscious ass. Remind yourself that you're seeking redemption today and wait until the aforementioned maid touches your arm. Girl, you say and she smiles. You symbolize a way out. Besides you're wearing your lucky shoes[2].

Take her back to your flat. Afterward she'll ask to have a shower and take a long time in the bathroom. Let her linger. She doesn't have a lot of personal space wherever she's living. She's lucky if she has a room of her own. Listen to her complaints about her employer. Let her miss her life in the Philippines. She's

---

[2] Ferragamo loafers. Once, in a bar in Lan Kwai Fong, an older woman clutching a large gin and tonic asked you if she could touch them. That's another story.

supporting a family of ten, minimum, back home. That's a lot of responsibility, even for a good girl.

Feed her something, she'll appreciate it, no one cooks for her. Two eggs, over easy, white toast. The secret is a combination of precise heat and patience. Sit at the kitchen table and watch her eat. You can tell a lot about a woman by the way she eats. Does she cut and scoop? Dip the yoke dry? Squash the eggs between the toasts and eat it like a sandwich?

If she talks about God, don't grimace; it's Sunday. Be polite, make small talk. Nod when she says she's never done this before. Neither have you.

When it's time to go, walk her downstairs to the lobby. Give her money for a taxi knowing that she won't take one, choosing instead to walk downhill to Statue Square and meet up with her friends again. Whatever you do, don't give out your cellphone number. Remember what happened last time.

Go back upstairs to your flat. Shower again. Change the sheets.

Watch *Blade Runner* on DVD. Watch up to the scene where Sean Young arrives in a fur coat, mascara pooling beneath those grieving eyes. Harrison Ford shoves her against the venetian blinds, her eyes widen and she flinches. Watch the scene repeatedly. You already know how the story ends: high above a futuristic city, Rutger Hauer, wearing blue underpants, morphs into a gargoyle.

Turn off the lights.

Step onto your balcony and smoke a joint. Remind yourself to go to bed by two o'clock, you have a busy week ahead. The Big Boss is flying in from New York. Scan the glowing windows of the city. It's lights-out most everywhere except for the girl in the tower overlooking the Botanical Gardens. She exercises in skimpy clothing late Sunday evenings, talks to herself, works something out elliptically.

Your telescope locks easily into place.

You can't stop yourself.

FAST EDDY

I STEP OUT INTO the rain-damp street for some air. At the end of Old Peak Road, off-duty taxi drivers congregate in the cul-de-sac. Drivers sprawl across car hoods while others polish fenders with rags. Still others squat together, smoking and talking.

Across the street from my building, I see the flicking headlights of the last cab in the stand at Hillsborough Court. I can't make out the driver's face, just the pale glow of his shirt and his beckoning hand. Just a couple drinks. Nothing more.

"Foreign Correspondents' Club," I say. He nods as if it's the only logical destination for a Caucasian man standing out on a Hong Kong street at midnight. I gaze over grimy rooftops stabilized by immense neon signs. The taxi descends and the signs rush up to meet me. Near the halfway point, they glare at me for one jarringly beautiful moment. There's a humming in my chest then the taxi hurtles around the next corner and the sensation is lost. I try to ignore the dangerous thrill as I drop through the neon snarl of the bar district. It has been a while and I miss the rush. Reminds me of amphetamines.

By the time I reach the bottom of the street the neon signs flash high above and, even though I tilt my head, they blur into an incomprehensible series of dots and dashes. Morse code isn't supposed to exist in the modern world, an outdated method made as obsolete as colonialism.

I fight the urge to rub my eyes and try, instead, to focus on the familiar pink martini glass that tips itself over next to the Foreign Correspondents' Club. The FCC. Booze is cheap and you don't have to be a journalist to join, as long as you're offered membership.

The taxi swerves to an abrupt halt in the middle of Lower Albert Street and delivers me face first into the vinyl headrest in front. I dab for blood on my forehead. Nothing. The driver grins in the plastic-slotted shadows of the front seat. "Okay, mister?" He points at the meter with his trigger finger then flips out his hand like a cellphone.

I come up with a couple good insults but figure it isn't worth my while. I'd just confuse him. That would be unsatisfying on this particular night, this anniversary of sorts. Instead, I hand over a large bill and, once he has provided change, pocket his tip. For a split second his smile freezes and then he inclines his head toward the tipping martini. Full. Empty.

"I wait?"

I ignore him and slam the door.

As I pick my way through oily puddles, I avoid a freewheeling bunch of drunken rugby fans celebrating a win at the Sevens' Tournament. Stepping into deep water, I douse my lucky shoes. I sense the dye weeping almost immediately, marking my sockless feet.

The bar is lined with a few familiar faces, most of which appear surprised to see me. I nod at a couple of Brits from Reuters and they scrape over my appearance, straight down to my dripping loafers, then ignore me. Some things never change. Harsh clove cigarette smoke gathers in the wood-hatched ceiling.

"Hey, Fast Eddy."

Joe, dependable Joe. He shoves at the worn rattan chair opposite his own, nods expectantly, and signals the waitress for a round. Fast Eddy, my Wan Chai name. I sit down. Remember the two-drink rule.

"Long time, no see. How's the banking business?" asks Joe automatically. He grins, his teeth painted with ancient coffee stains. Another rundown expatriate going local. Why doesn't he just make an appointment with a fucking dentist when he's on home leave like everybody else?

I shrug.

Joe laughs as if he doesn't really care, not true because he's an American and competitive by nature, then he launches into a story about a Cathay pilot who lives across the hall. I nod and smile every now and again, even laugh at the high point.

"Three bar girls. Don't that beat all." Joe slaps at his rumpled knee. His Adam's apple jerks up and down the tanned column of his neck as he downs a glass of San Miguel in one slow gulp. Empty. Full. I don't stop my hand from signalling for another round and scan the exits. All clear.

Smoke twists and rolls within the wooden boxes on the ceiling, searching for an escape route. One frail arm of smoke reaches across a beam and joins hands with its neighbour before it disappears into the next crowded box, going nowhere together.

It's funny how I search the crowded streets for familiar faces, how I never see anyone I know. Sure, I spot a few Caucasians but no one familiar. The only places I'm certain to know someone are here or down on The Filthy Acre. The Acre is definitely off limits. The abrupt clink of bottles and glasses on a tray pulls me back to the table. So much for the two-drink rule.

"Okay, okay?" asks the waitress. The name on her badge reads "Merry!" *God rest ye merry gentlemen.* Most of the windows are open. A large scrum of rugby freaks staggers past, arms around one another. The street definitely sounds busier.

The door crashes open. Willis wanders in and leans against the bar right next to the front door. Great. One night out in ten months and my fucking dealer shows up. I wonder who sponsored his membership and at what cost.

Willis' glittering eyes track the crowd and he nods here and there without risking direct eye contact. High. Probably ecstasy. He unclenches his jaw and raises a vodka martini to his lips. Before long his gaze slides over, pauses, rewinds, and repeats the action. That's the only way I know he really notices me. The double slide. I also know what he's thinking: meet me in the bathroom. Score.

Ignore him.

I drag my attention back to the table and focus on Joe's mouth, count the words dropping off his chapped lips. Joe worries about the latest article he's shopping around, complains that no one appreciates his individual take on politics in China. This deteriorates into a lengthy contrast of the Chinese versus American political systems and no surprise, the Americans win.

Joe is an earnest American. I kind of like that about him, not that I'd admit it. Sure, he's loud and drones on and on about The

States. At least he believes in something and can say so in less than 1300 words when he's typing. That's what makes him one of the best, his old-school journalistic skills.

"Listen. A few of the boys are heading down to that girlie bar in Wan Chai, the one with the karaoke upstairs? What's the name? You know it. Why don't you — "

"No," I say. Difficult to do given the girlie bar in question, one of my favourites. It took me two months to get over rehab and another six/eight to fully wean myself off bar girls, using a combination of nightly workouts and extensive DVD viewing. "No" is one word I've repeated to myself so many times lately that I can't keep count anymore.

"C'mon, Fast Eddy, it'll do you good. It's been a tough year. I mean. Losing your job — "

"You heard what I said."

Joe levels his flat brown eyes on me. Wrinkles fan out from their margins before abruptly turning the corners of his long face. The whites of his eyes are faintly yellow, the sign of a steady drinker. Joe looks surprisingly good for a daily habit of ten beer and assorted gin tonics. He leans as far back in the chair as he can, clasps his hands together like some kind of preacher.

We consider one another.

"You want to talk about it?" He leans into the table. His hands spring apart and flex. I wonder if he might actually touch me or hit me. I don't know which is worse.

I shake my head. The wicker chair prickles my lower back, cane needles scratching my skin through my linen shirt. Little triggers. I crave a high, any high. When will it end? Willis twitches out of his shiny suit jacket and settles into his barstool.

A beer sign flickers and Willis' face in the mirror alternates between yellow and reptilian green.

"I'd talk to *you* about it, buddy," says Joe with the same certainty he brings to both politics and the newspaper business. This certainty reminds me of my sponsor. I consider my options. Stay and talk to Joe. Leave. There's no way I can leave with that jitney, Willis, barring the front door. I'll never make it past without his fare. As it stands I've barely made it through the longest twelve months of my life without him, a year even worse than that of my divorce.

I stare down into my sweating glass and think again about my sponsor. I think about the program. Pause on Step Five: admit to another being the exact nature of your wrongs. My wrongs. I've never told anyone. It figures. I'm working the program in a fucking bar.

෨ ෨ ෨

The beat throbbed hot-pink airplane-strip lighting across the crowded dance floor. A heady combination of sex, sweat, and expectations. Fast Eddy was barely concentrating. Hard bodies everywhere. Fan-fucking-tastic.

These Filipinas are too lovely. Long hair, short hair, tight jeans, but look at them sideways and they're pregnant. He groped his back pocket for condoms. Check.

Shit, stuck with The Old Fat Businessman. The OFB. At least the OFB scored the best seat in the house, beside the front window and next to the entrance. First to scope out the action both on the street and on the dance floor.

"Heineken?" Big cheese in town, Eddy. Show him a good time, Eddy. The pitch had gone unbelievably well, considering the shitty book the junior associates threw together, last minute. After dinner, the OFB wanted to check out local hospitality and Fast Eddy's name came up. Guess money can buy anything. Even me.

"No, thanks," the OFB answered. "Jet lag."

An awkward silence. Fast Eddy carefully pulled the foil label from the bottle neck. Drinking beer? He doesn't even like it, slows him down too much. Red Bull's more his style when he's rolling through The Filthy Acre, his final destination following this feeble attempt at entertaining a fat fuck.

"Maybe I'll have something to eat," said the OFB. "Any suggestions?"

Is this guy for real? Fucking hard bodies crawling all over the place and he wants a crappy burger? Just then a sweet-smelling, long-legged beauty wafted in the door, her red-silk cheongsam so short he spied the lacy white cheeks of her ass. I'd eat that. Maybe later. After he tucked the OFB into bed.

"Gosh." The OFB's eyes opened wide. In the stabbing flash of the strobe lights, his ears glowed red, redder, red, redder. Fast Eddy watched the tip of the OFB's tongue lick at pink prawn lips.

"You like?" Fast Eddy nodded in the red-silk hard body's direction.

"Oh. No. I'm a married man. A happily married man. My wife — "

"Isn't here."

As the OFB rattled off his itinerary, his eyes never left the red-silk hard body. He counted off the attractions he must visit while in Hong Kong, a list no doubt provided by his wife. An excellent cook, judging by the OFB's generously padded physique.

"I have to see the Peak and ride the Star Ferry and is there a junk trip I can go on?"

Sounded like a guidebook. Middle-of-the-road guidebook, probably Fodor's. Good Christ Almighty. Fast Eddy stifled a moist beer yawn and agreed to escort the OFB to Sai Kung for a seafood lunch. Most lovely. Sunday, say eleven o'clock?

"Um, how old do you think that girl is?" asked the OFB as if he couldn't stop himself.

"Old enough. Let me set you up." Well, well, there's life in the OFB after all.

Easing a moist finger along the carefully pressed collar of his khaki tropical-weight, mail-order shirt, the OFB stared at his water bottle for a long moment. One of the fine muscles above Fast Eddy's right eye fluttered before settling into a steady beat in unison with the music.

"Lovely girl." The OFB's eyes flooded with eagerness.

"A lot to handle." Fast Eddy nodded as slow as possible. Hard to do when high. "Yes sir, there are days when even a young guy like myself can't . . . " Words drifted away and he lifted his shoulders into what felt like a casual shrug.

"Oh. My. Yes."

Fast Eddy patted his right breast pocket like a baby. "Thank God, I've got what I need." His eyebrows arched into his forehead. Maybe the amphetamine wasn't such a good idea but he needed something extra to make it through the evening. He counted four full beats of the music. Counting usually helped him come down, soothed him.

Eight half-beats later, the OFB asked what he meant and Fast Eddy offered Viagra. The OFB considered the blue pills over one quarter beat then swallowed. Half an hour later, Fast

Eddy beckoned the red-silk hard body over and explained what was required. They negotiated a price and she led the flushed schoolboy version of the OFB off to the bathroom for stall delights unlike anything he had encountered before.

Fast Eddy tried relaxing into his barstool and absentmindedly swallowed an ecstasy tablet. It wasn't long before the missed beat of the techno blues provided him with the space he needed to linger inside the music. Beautiful. He watched the slow motion movements of the dancers and imagined the blowjob the OFB was getting. Around-the-world. Definitely more than the old man bargained for. Fast Eddy was rock hard thinking about it.

People flowed onto the crowded dance floor, leaving neon trails behind them like a long exposure photograph. He attempted to capture their ecstatic grainy faces and contrast them against the static background. Increased shutter speed. Gave up. Panned the vibrating crowd and started counting.

The music pulsated from one song to the next, beats blurred into a tangled mass of rhythms. The relentless drumbeats inhabited his body, moving him from side to side. His jaw ached with pleasure.

Fast Eddy turned toward the open front door and caught a glimpse of a crowd surging. Swivelled back toward the tinted windows facing the street and watched a black-and-white swirl of people push their way down the narrow street. Spindly arms rose above heads in a futile wave, attempted to make space. Going nowhere together.

Hallucinating?

He rubbed his eyes.

No.

Definitely a mob.

Scrolled his memory for mention of demonstrations. He couldn't recall reading about any authorized demonstrations in the SCMP and he always checked. Crowds scared the shit out of him, ever since he was trapped in Lan Kwai Fong during New Year's Eve celebrations.

Illegal demonstration? Falun Gong?

No placards or political T-shirts. Just everyday people carrying plastic bags brimming with fruits and vegetables above their heads. Rugby followers wearing a variety of brightly coloured sports jerseys. This was a spontaneous mob. He ignored the gummy lump stuck to his tongue.

The crowd lurched forward, emitted a metallic energy that radiated in acidic waves and penetrated the filtered windows. Replicated back onto the base of his skull. A loudspeaker stuttered in Cantonese. Stifled shouts bounced off glass-fronted buildings then Fast Eddy caught a whiff of sulphur.

In that moment the crowd rioted. People flailed their scrawny arms and started beating each other about the head and shoulders. They shouted, shoved, and twisted themselves together into a locked puzzle. A series of windy shouts knocked at the windows, rattled the doors.

Gotta get out of here. Visually tracked his getaway across the packed dance floor to the back. Zeroed in on the tower of sealed wooden liquor boxes that blocked the alley exit. If the crowd forced their way in. Trampled to death.

Time shifted. Fast Eddy watched a pasty hand close the door, fumble with chrome locks, before he realized it was his hand, attached to his numb arm, that snapped the locks. He was certain he heard them thunk shut, impossible over the pounding music.

Fast Eddy

The bouncers arrived on his heels, nodded at him and jammed a board through the door handles. They linked arms, created a human fence across the blocked front doorway and eyed the dancers. Transmitted steel-edged warnings.

Going nowhere. Nowhere.

Relax. Don't panic.

The DJ cut the music and repeated that everyone needed to keep quiet and stand still. His authoritative voice echoed through the uneasy room. Even the stoned dancers stopped moving. A humid, earthy scent pressed down from the baffle ceiling, then somebody turned the air conditioning on full blast, thank God.

Fast Eddy couldn't take his eyes off the moving mosaic caught in the window frame. He focused on the unremarkable face of a young woman wearing a ponytail. Shielding herself from her neighbours' blows as efficiently as possible. Blank-faced, she laboured against a force that pulled her like trash into a flooded gutter.

The shouting intensified.

Fast Eddy envisioned black, lacquered batons swinging among the flapping arms and they appeared like magic. Yes. Policemen edged a path with their scratched plastic riot shields, methodically battering heads and shoulders. Fast Eddy caught a glimpse of a white-haired old woman with blood running down one cheek, her tattered cardigan hung off a shoulder, exposing a paper-thin undershirt.

Un-fucking-believable.

A pair of hands shoved him against the inside of the window, hard.

"What the?" Peeled himself off the glass and spun around.

The OFB stood there wheezing, thinning hair flattened against perspiring temples. Glassy eyes darted from side to side. "I oughtta hit you, you bastard."

"Listen, old man."

"Don't call me old man."

"You are an old man. Listen. There's a riot." Fast Eddy gestured. So much for keeping the client happy.

"I'm an old man. At least. You. You're despicable." The OFB took an unsteady breath. "You got that. That girl. To stick her tongue. Up my ass. What's wrong with you?"

Good question. He thought about articulating an apology. Typed and counted the words. Why should he apologize? The OFB was like any middle-aged, married Caucasian man in Southeast Asia. When presented with temptation they always picked the ripest. "Look. There's a riot going on. We've gotta stay calm."

That's when the OFB stared out the window. He slowly shook his head. Opened and closed his mouth a few times and fixed Fast Eddy with red-rimmed eyes. "This place is crazy. You're crazy."

"Screw you. Fat loser." Fucking fat wallets. Buying everything and everybody, including the crimson hard body that should've been his for the evening. He'd seen her first. Finders keepers. Fast Eddy felt his high slipping away, replaced by familiar anxiety crackling beneath his skin like liquid silver.

"Fat," said the OFB.

Fast Eddy thought the OFB didn't look quite right; something about the older man's face reminded him of ashtray contents. He bore no traces of his former ruddy complexion. "Calm down."

The OFB swore then kneaded his neck and shoulder. Sweat soaked through his faded hair and dripped down, pooled into his collar.

"You all right, old man? You don't look so good."

"I think I'm gonna be si — " The OFB vomited down his chest and onto the slick tile floor. A greasy mixture of partially digested food and beer splattered onto Fast Eddy's shoes.

Viagra heart attack, thought Fast Eddy. He hustled the OFB into a chair and shouted at the bouncers. "Call an ambulance! *Giu gau seung che! Giu gau seung che!*"

It took a few slow minutes to maneuver the OFB out to one of the many waiting ambulances because, although the riot had ceased, the crowd took its time thinning out. Fast Eddy pushed to the front of the injury queue, caused a scene, insisted the OFB receive treatment first, handed over a bribe. A sullen paramedic ushered the old man up steep stairs into the waiting ambulance.

Fast Eddy spent time assuring the OFB that he'd call the office and the wife as soon as possible. Let them both know the old man has been transported to hospital. Tried to disregard the vomit stains on his lucky shoes.

"God, I wish I was — "

Fast Eddy ignored the OFB. He couldn't tolerate the pukey, sweaty smell. An amphetamine headache was forming behind his left eye. He slipped past several moaning people receiving first aid and then the police pacing next to a cordoned-off, yellow-tarped mound.

The detectives arrived, lifted up the crinkly plastic covering. A woman with a ponytail sprawled face first on the sidewalk, her Burberry knock-off skirt flipped up above the waist, exposing scuffed white underpants.

The detectives talked before they wandered away, synthetic wood clipboards in hand. They left her there, half-naked, out in the open. No one seemed to notice. People drifted past with little more than a cursory glance.

Fast Eddy wondered who would cover him in the street if he lay dead. He smoothed his shirt and fingered the hem. He beckoned to a police officer and pointed out that the woman remained uncovered. The constable said he should mind his own business, move along.

"But she's been stepped on." As if that explained anything.

"Okay, okay," said the other constable, who then scrutinized his identification card before dismissing him with a flick of his leather motorcycle-gloved hand.

కళకళ

"What was the fat businessman so upset about?" asks Joe.

"Probably the Viagra. Too much for him." I widen my dry eyes in an attempt not to look away, especially to the left. Liars usually glance to the left.

I rattle on about the political bullshit at Goldman Sachs, about how it was just as well I was fired. About how I should've quit last year when they screwed me out of my bonus but that's how it goes. Yadda, yadda, yadda.

Joe listens without interrupting.

"New job's okay. Scotiabank's a good bank," I say when I can't think of another thing.

"Did you cover her?"

I glance at him through the spicy haze.

Joe nods and slowly fidgets a coaster into shreds. His gaze lingers on my face as if he's memorizing every feature.

BLANK

MIDNIGHT AT THE bank.

When the door of the half-lit conference room opens, it's Jerry, smartass senior vice-president with a golden touch. The youngest senior VP in the history of Morgan Stanley. In his late thirties, Jerry lives alone in an isolated house high above Big Wave Bay, an exclusive expatriate enclave, his sailboat anchored in the waters below. Jerry's a legend in the investment banking world; mergers and acquisitions are his specialty.

I stand at attention for a moment and sit again.

Ignoring me, Jerry slumps into an office chair at the conference table. Beneath the glare of a pot light, his sun-scarred face is made up of large, irregular features like pieces of a broken platter, reassembled and glued. His gaze is piercing blue. Jerry asks, "Best punk band?"

"The Clash."

"Best song?"

"Guns of Brixton."

"Unusual choice, Blank. That'll do. Someone told me you were in the army."

"The Rangers, sir."

"Where did you tour?" Jerry glances at his watch.

"Afghanistan, sir. Two tours."

"You should know I'm an anarchist and I don't fucking believe in war." Jerry cocks his head to one side and the other.

I consider his broken face, alternating with light and shadow like thermal imaging. "I don't know that I believe in it either."

Afghanistan. It's been four years. Each night I scramble across a field of dry, scratchy grasses. Tony's waiting beneath a blackened tree. That's when I wake. Colours, trails, sounds vibrating. Never mind.

"You all right, Blank?"

"Yes, sir. The flight knocked it out of me."

"Call me Jerry. Now tell me about DoubleClick."

"That was a tricky one, Jerry."

"Yeah, I've got tricky. Really tricky."

A deal I helped broker, DoubleClick is an online advertising company acquired by Google. We put together a compelling deal, stole it from Microsoft at the last minute.

"How'd you get Google to up their offer?"

"I reminded them that they needed to win the war against Microsoft."

"You guys and your fucking wars." Jerry crosses his arms across his chest. He stares out the windows that overlook the harbour. Outside, the buildings are lit up with a sea of lights floating like colour static and, at this time of night, it's darker inside than outside.

I wait.

I've heard through the grapevine that Jerry is busy drumming up a new account he will not identify for fear of jinxing the deal. He's superstitious.

Jerry swivels back to the table and says, "I'm putting together a pitch book for CRITIC." CRITIC is the largest state-owned investment company of the People's Republic of China. If we're successful and sign them as a client, there'd be a neverending stream of work for the bank. A huge prize.

Silence pools on the tabletop.

"What's your strategy?" I defer to his judgment and use the time to think about the company. I don't know much. CRITIC's primarily known for mergers and acquisitions, with a focus on foreign investments, technology, and best practices in operations and management.

"What would you focus on, Blank?"

"Technology."

Jerry says, "That'll do. DoubleClick was a helluva pitch, Blank. A helluva pitch. I need you here as my right hand. Two weeks. We'll build the pitch book together. And we'll use DoubleClick as a case study."

"Yes, sir."

"We'll start in the morning, this conference room. We need to re-key the door — I'll make the arrangements and get the key to you. It'll just be the two of us so get ready for paperwork. I'll bring my own printer, no routing through the office. We've got to be fucking careful, Blank."

I nod. All of a sudden I'm too tired to speak after the sixteen-hour flight from New York.

Abruptly, Jerry exits the conference room, slams the door on the way out. A minute later loud music shrieks from his corner office. Jerry's dedication to first wave punk is notorious.

I drag my suitcase across the marble floor to the front lobby. A personal assistant in a black pantsuit materializes out of the shadows and arranges for a car service to the Harbourview Hotel. I know I won't sleep. Everything new, moving and vibrating.

ల ల ల

"That's enough work," says Jerry late the next afternoon.

I push aside the document I'm reading. The conference table is covered with piles of paper. We're building a complicated pitch book. Multiple tech companies, each with summaries of product lines, details on financial performance, capital structure, valuation parameters; a large amount of information to analyze.

"You play poker, Blank?" asks Jerry.

"Yes, sir."

"I run a Saturday game. C'mon out and I'll introduce you to the guys." Jerry scrawls the directions to his house in Big Wave Bay, includes his personal cellphone number. "Don't hand it out to anyone, *especially* Worley Man."

Mr. Worley is the managing director of the Hong Kong office but I haven't met him yet; he's away on a business trip inside China. I agree to the poker game and head back in the direction I think will take me to my temporary office.

"Yeah, turn left and you're there," calls Jerry from behind. "Get with the ticket, Blank."

ల ల ల

Red taxis inch past, tail lights piercing airborne particulate. I cover my mouth when I cross the street. The sidewalks are too crowded so I balance along the curb. In a noodle shop people huddle over bowls of steaming food, chopsticks flashing. Bones. A pneumatic drill punctures concrete alongside a barricade with amber lights. I startle. Breathe long slow breaths, in and out, through my mouth.

Blank

On the bus I find a seat on the upper level, at the front, a birds' eye view over the street. The bus careens through the city into a white-tiled tunnel. Strip fluorescent lighting pulls the bus through. We emerge into the green southside. The bus sways along a narrow coastal road. Shotcrete walls line the sides. Every now and again, the bus catches up to a cyclist and passes quickly, before braking into a corner, and another, and another. I'm suddenly nauseated by the staggering movement and stumble to the lower level. I lean my forehead against the cold air-conditioned window. I don't want to close my eyes but I cannot help it.

The Shek-O minibus is packed with families loaded down with beach equipment: shade umbrellas, coolers, and brightly coloured bags overflowing with toys and food. Standing room only, except for the last open seat next to me. The driver leans on the steering wheel and studies his folded newspaper, checking the stock market.

An old guy dressed in a Speedo and swim cap, a faded towel draped over his shoulder, and flip-flops, boards the bus. He's talking on his cellphone and eyes the empty seat beside me. I edge closer to the wall and make space. The old guy ignores me. When more people board the bus, he curses under his breath and sits on the edge of my seat.

When the bus is crammed the driver takes off at high speed. The road is narrower, still. Wind whistles through open windows. I cannot move. Everyone is talking at once, louder and louder, until I can no longer hear myself think. I'm fuzzy from a combination of fatigue and jet lag.

It's difficult to believe I exited a city of eight million less than an hour ago. I've taken 100 mental screen shots over that time. Congested streets, taxis swerving, cyclists with knees flashing, an old man in a Speedo talking on his cellphone. All tamped down by heat and humidity.

The minibus swerves into a small parking lot that serves as the terminus of Big Wave Bay Road. It squeals to a halt. The crowd straggles down a narrow road past overflowing garbage bins. Disappears in the direction of the beach. I'm the last passenger to step down onto pavement.

The parking lot overflows with cars. I scan the perimeter. There are no people except for an elderly couple who squat in the shade of a banyan. The man holds his head in his hands and appears to be sleeping. The woman sits with her knees far apart and stares down at her faded slippers. Close by the couple is a small, white sign with a gold number. There it is. Number nine.

The gate is tall, ornate, tarnished gold-and-black. Two dust-streaked Grecian urns perch on gateposts. A small, black speaker box juts out of the ground. I press the red button and wait.

"That you, Blank?"

"Yes, sir."

"One question."

"Shoot."

"Best punk band you've seen live?" Static snarls over the intercom.

I consider his question. "Green Day."

"That is an absolute shit band, Blank."

The gate slowly swings open.

I walk up the long, curving driveway through the shade of tree branches that meet above the road, a flickering green cathedral. Alive. I round a final corner and there is the house. It is white with a grey-tiled roof and a wraparound verandah, and faces the South China Sea.

The house sits high atop a granite headland; white metal railings hold it away from the cliff edge. The view is spectacular. In the distance, small islands emerge through a dull haze. The sea is deceptively calm from this height, a deep dark blue. I think I hear the faint roar of surf but it could be fatigue.

A motorcycle and a black Mercedes sedan are carelessly parked in the wide driveway. I cross a lawn staggered with flagstones to an open door on the deep verandah. I hear voices. I enter without knocking and follow the sound of men playing cards to a sun-filled room in the back.

Four men sit in varying degrees of disarray, propped up by their elbows. The card table is scattered with red, white, and blue poker chips. The side table is full of dirty glasses and half-empty bottles of gin, vodka, and whiskey. A ceiling fan slowly moves the air around.

I take a seat at the table.

Jerry introduces the men. Chef, a Belgian who works at a country club; Load Toad, an Englishman with a trading company; and, Zubis, a well-groomed Canadian who owns a string of restaurants in the entertainment district.

The men nod over their cards.

"How long have you guys been at it?"

Zubis checks his watch and says, "11:00 AM."

"Blank's the next Golden Boy," Jerry says and pushes his long dirty-blond hair off his brow. His forehead is paler than the rest of his nut-brown face.

"Not true," I say even though it's true. I want it; need it, more than I've ever verbalized. At twenty-nine years of age, I'm the same age Jerry was when he made senior vice-president. No. VP can't come soon enough.

"Yeah, it's true," says Jerry ruefully.

I survey the living room. The space contains little. An oversized sectional with colourful pillows, and a large canvas of abstract art resting casually against the wall. An oversized ornate mirror is propped against the other. The hardwood floor is bare.

"Great stereo." I nod at electronics.

"I listen to records on big-ass speakers," says Jerry and throws poker chips in the pot.

"That a Linn?" asks Load Toad.

Jerry nods. "Akurate. With WATT/Puppy speakers."

"The speakers remind me of Darth Vader," I say.

"Blank, I'm your father," says Jerry and laughs.

"Records. That's brilliant. Reminds me of the old days at the Factory," says Load Toad.

"House music," says Jerry and snorts.

"Different strokes, eh, Jerry? No. The Factory was fucking brilliant. Wonderful music, mates and days. You know, I curse myself for taking it for granted," says Load Toad.

"You ever been to Ibiza, Load Toad?" asks Chef.

"Yeah. Me and my mates used to head down, now and again. Stay up all night Friday, Saturday. Pass out cold on the plane on the way back. Christ, I can't do that anymore," says Load Toad.

"Always wanted to go," says Chef. "Pass the olives."

The air is filled with cigarette smoke even though the windows are wide open to the patio. Outside, water gurgles in a pond tamped down with broad-leafed lily pads and neon-orange carp break the surface. Beyond the patio is a lush garden that has gone wild. Fiery blooms hang from branches of a tree I don't recognize. The breeze pushes fern-like branches and blooms trail.

Beyond the garden lies a steep, rock-covered hillside. A line of hikers traverses the mountain's spine, their brightly coloured hats trailing down, before disappearing into the scrubby brush. I hear the call of birds hiding in the vegetation.

"Caught any snakes lately, Jerry?" asks Zubis.

"One last week. The gardener's on watch."

"Did you kill it?"

"Nah. The gardener threw it in a basket and took it somewhere."

"He probably sold it at the wet market," says Load Toad. "Snake soup has curative properties, eh."

"I've tasted it," says Chef. "A little chewy, but not bad."

"Christ, is there anything you've eaten that you haven't liked?" asks Load Toad.

"No," says Chef.

The men settle into play.

Chef wins several hands in a row.

"Chef, you're on fucking fire," says Jerry and throws down his cards in disgust.

"Meh, it's nothing," says Chef. He slaps his heavy arms like he's trying to increase his circulation. There are splatter burns on his forearms, small red craters. Scars.

"You should taste his food," Zubis says to me. "He's a genius."

"I just write the menu, manage the kitchen. I miss cooking real food for real people," says Chef.

The men play poker until shadows lengthen in the garden.

"Fancy some seafood?" asks Load Toad.

"Curry with prawns. I know a place." Chef rubs his bald head like he's polishing a stainless-steel bowl.

ॐॐॐ

Jerry pulls a battered green Jaguar out of the garage and we all pile in. Zubis rides shotgun while Load Toad, Chef and I crowd the backseat. It's a tight fit.

"Still driving this piece of shit," says Zubis.

"It's functional, isn't it?" says Jerry. "Besides, I'm giving it to the man."

Load Toad nudges me and says, "Ask him what man."

"What man?"

"Some wanker I won it off in a poker game," says Jerry and smirks in the rearview.

"Don't remind me," says Zubis drily. "Are you at least maintaining the engine?"

"I want you to know that I don't care," says Jerry. "But yes, yes, I am."

"Watch out for the minibus," says Zubis.

"Cheffie, you're crushing me," says Load Toad. He squirms in his seat.

"Sorry, sorry," says Chef and shifts his weight. "You ever see a skinny chef?"

"No, sir," I say.

"You ever do, don't eat in his restaurant."

"Or hers," says Load Toad. "Equal opportunity and such."

"Of course, of course. The kitchen is open to everyone." Chef makes a sweeping motion like he's pushing a curtain aside with his hand.

Zubis says, "I heard you're sleeping with the head pastry chef over at The Peninsula, Chef."

"We're friends," says Chef. His ears redden more.

Jerry accelerates rapidly. The car jitters into oncoming traffic, overtakes a minibus and swerves to safety at the last moment.

Horns sound and the minibus driver waves both arms out the window.

Zubis grips the armrest. His knuckles are white.

"Take that, you bastard," shouts Load Toad. He shoves his head out the window and glares back. His hair is whirling around his head, bushy sideburns a tangled mess. He drops back into his seat with a whoosh. "I hate minibus drivers."

I laugh. It feels good. I can't remember the last time I laughed.

"But seriously, Chef. How do you do it?" asks Jerry. "I've met her and she's fucking gorgeous."

"It's nothing, nothing," says Chef.

"C'mon, Cheffie," says Load Toad and pats his hair down with pudgy hands. The effort is futile. "Out with it."

"We share a certain interest," says Chef carefully.

"Christ, not the spanking again," says Load Toad and groans.

"You don't understand. I'm under a lot of pressure in the kitchen," says Chef. His voice is plaintive. "And I like to be told what to do."

"Be careful," says Zubis.

"She's over in TST," says Chef. "The wife will never know."

"I know," says Zubis.

"Yeah, but you've got inside information, on account of your connections," says Load Toad.

Zubis gives Load Toad a dirty look and says, "Hong Kong's a small town. People gossip."

"Is this about sex? You know, Europeans are more relaxed about sex," says Chef. He drums his sausage-like fingers on his tanned knee.

"It's not about sex. It's about discretion," says Zubis.

"Yeah, this is why I don't believe in marriage," says Jerry.

At a fork in the road Jerry veers abruptly to the left, passing the golf course at high speed. In the distance a trio of golfers tee up. The grass glows electric, greener than the surrounding vegetation, surreal. Jerry's driving faster and faster, weaving between lanes, straddling the centre line. Floating on a cushion of air.

Then we brake through a traffic circle and arrive at Shek-O with a jerk. There's no space in the public lot. Jerry double-parks in front of a tourist shop that overflows with rolls of rattan beach mats.

"Exactly how am I supposed to get out?" asks Zubis.

"Throw a leg over, old man," says Jerry and holds open his door.

"I'm not old." Zubis scrambles over the gearshift and emerges on the driver side. His blue linen shorts catch, rip along the side seam. "Jesus, Jerry. My shorts are ruined."

Chef leads the way down a quiet side street to a nondescript local restaurant, a favourite by the looks of it. It's packed. The patio is illuminated with a combination of strip fluorescent lighting and strings of white Christmas lights tucked under the frayed awning.

After we settle into a table, Chef proceeds to order dish after dish of seafood and fresh fish: prawns and hairy crabs and whitefish. We feast, we cannot stop ourselves, and cold beer flows. All of a sudden I'm exhausted.

"Jet lag's a bastard," says Load Toad as Jerry deposits me into a cab. I fall asleep on the drive back into the city. When I awake the next morning, I have a hazy memory of walking through the hotel lobby, back to my room with its harbour view and, for a moment, I wonder if it's real.

❧❧❧

Jerry and I work hard that first week, late into the night. At the end of each workday I return to the hotel to sleep as best I can. What a joke. Midnight on Black Rock Hill. Never mind.

Late Thursday afternoon I ask, "Where did you meet the guys you play poker with, Jerry?"

"There's a pub in SoHo called The Globe. Great place with little tabletop jukeboxes. I'll take you sometime."

"What's on tap?"

"A real mix. San Miguel, Jaipur, Old Speckled Hen. It changes."

"Sounds good."

Jerry drains his cup of coffee and says, "Listen, Blank. It's a good idea to have friends outside the office. Bankers are a buncha assholes. Speaking of, I'm having dinner with Worley Man tonight and you're coming. Eight o'clock, the Kathmandu Restaurant on Old Bailey Street."

❧❧❧

The dining room of the Kathmandu is narrow and dark. A pair of yellow eyes, stencilled with kohl, stares at me from the wall above the reception desk. Tapestries hang from the walls and burnished objects of art rest in little niches.

I edge past a group of Gurkhas, some in their jackets, some in their shirt sleeves, drinking together at the small bar. They're celebrating, uniformed arms raised, saluting one another. "Nepalese holiday," says the owner and shrugs apologetically.

The restaurant consists of a single line of tables covered with roughly-hewn tablecloths, and a narrow aisle. The walls are covered with blue paint so dark and flat, it absorbs the small amount of light cast by candles. I can hear the cooks working but cannot see them. Clanging metal.

"Over here, *Green Day*," calls Jerry. He stands and points at a chair opposite. Unfortunately I'm facing the back of the restaurant, exposed. Never mind.

Jerry introduces Mrs. Worley, a preternaturally pale woman with straw-like, bleached-blonde hair fashionably cut at a sharp, irregular angle. A sensitive face. She wears a white slip dress, her undergarments visible through the flimsy material. She glows in the dark of the restaurant.

"Mike Blank. How d'you do?"

"I'm wonderful, Mike," she says, her voice as bright as her hazel-green eyes. "Mr. Worley assures me he's on his way. He's called and said he's walking down to the taxi stand, this very minute."

"Let's order a few appetizers while we wait for the old man," says Jerry.

"I've had Indian, of course. How is Nepalese any different?" Mrs. Worley asks.

"The spices."

"What spices?"

"Nepalese spices."

"And what exactly are Nepalese spices?" asks Mrs. Worley.

"I don't know and I don't care. They're fucking delicious," says Jerry. Mrs. Worley laughs, throwing her head back and exposing her long, vulnerable neck. When she laughs, her whole body relaxes.

"You're funny, Jerry."

"It's a fucking mystery. Forget the CIA holed up in The Manhattan out in Tai Tam, tracking digital info out of Mainland China, we've got Nepalese spices," says Jerry.

"There are CIA in Hong Kong?" I ask.

"Yeah. American guys who work on contract, never talk about their jobs, and speak Putahongua like a fucking taxi driver. Just listen and you'll know," says Jerry.

"Who?" asks Mrs. Worley.

"Lippincott."

"I didn't know." Mrs. Worley's voice is full of wonder.

The appetizers arrive. Mrs. Worley tells stories of her two years in Hong Kong, urban hiking in the city and surrounding parks, tours around Asia with the American Women's Association. "We're here for a few more years and then we're definitely going back to New York," she says and sips sparkling water.

"Have a samosa," says Jerry and slips a flaky triangle onto Mrs. Worley's empty plate. She nibbles the edges of her pastry before abandoning it.

When Mr. Worley calls for directions, Jerry tells him we'll wait on the street for him to arrive. We excuse ourselves from the table and head outside, crossing the street to a large, uniformly grey building that leans back from the sidewalk. From this vantage point, we have a clear view up and down the steep street.

"This is a jail, decommissioned now. It's a heritage building, not that it would stop the property developers. The fuckers," says Jerry and pats the brick wall. Three handmade brooms are wedged behind a drainpipe, their bristles aimed downhill at an unknown target.

The front of the Kathmandu is made of a panel of French doors propped open to the evening breeze, and there are gold flickers of candlelight. The Gurkhas have pushed together two large tables and taken over the front of the house. A few are standing at the bar, talking and drinking. When the owner delivers a tray of drinks, one breaks into song and the rest immediately stop what they're doing and stand facing the Nepalese flag, singing together in one voice. Brothers in arms.

"Who are they here with?"

"They probably work security for Li Ka-Shing. He must be out of the country for them all to have the night off." Jerry paces into the street and stares downhill toward the Mid-Levels escalator. There's no sign of the elusive Mr. Worley.

"There must be thirty guys, maybe more."

"He and his family travel around Hong Kong with a sizable detail ever since their son was kidnapped in the '90s. Gurkhas are short but tough. I wouldn't cross them."

"They're fierce soldiers in the field."

"You miss the army, Blank?"

"No, sir. I do not."

That's when we see him. A man strides purposefully up the stairs that run alongside the escalator. It's Mr. Worley. He wears a grey suit and dress shoes. He also wears thick, steel-rimmed eyeglasses. When he sees us, he cuts across the street on the diagonal.

"This is Mike Blank. He's here to help with CRITIC." Jerry gestures in my direction.

Mr. Worley wordlessly shakes my hand and asks Jerry. "How goes the battle?"

"The pitch is coming together. Blank is a working like — "

"I've got bad news. My source tells me Lehman's putting together a pitch for CRITIC too."

"You've got a spy inside Lehman's?" asks Jerry.

"Of course."

Jerry swears.

"What are you going to do, Jerry?"

"Multiple pitches," says Jerry, thinking out loud.

Mr. Worley nods once abruptly, turns on his heel, and strides into the restaurant.

"We'll get there," I say, even though I have no idea what I'm talking about.

"I've been working on getting one meeting with CRITIC for six months. Six fucking months. Can you stay longer than two weeks, Blank?" asks Jerry and scratches his head.

"Yes, sir." There's nothing holding me in New York beyond an apartment I can easily sublet and I want the chance to prove myself. I need to succeed. Besides, this account could land me a VP position. Definitely.

We stand in the dark street for a few minutes and talk about next steps with CRITIC, brainstorm how to approach the expanded pitch. "Email me those strategies and we'll get started right away. Yeah, and remind me to find you an executive apartment. The Harbourview has no fucking soul," says Jerry as we make our way back into the restaurant.

Mr. and Mrs. Worley aren't speaking when we take our seats at the table, and the air is filled with expectations. From their body language it's clear they haven't finished their argument.

When Jerry places their food orders Mrs. Worley says, "I miss New York."

"I don't know when we'll get back," says Mr. Worley. His voice is brusque, businesslike. He jams his Blackberry into his jacket pocket.

"Where are you living?" I ask. The question feels random and I don't know why I ask except to change the subject, avoid the tension.

"A milkshake-pink building on top of that hill," Mrs. Worley says and waves a pale hand in a westward direction.

"Parkview. I need a drink," says Mr. Worley.

"I'm not supposed to drink," says Mrs. Worley.

"Who said anything about a drink?" Mr. Worley says.

When the food arrives, hot and steaming, Mrs. Worley inhales deeply and says, "Mmmm, mysterious Nepalese spices." Everyone laughs except for Mr. Worley who is surreptitiously viewing the wine list, squinting at the folder in the dark. Myopic.

ॐॐॐ

I transfer to an executive suite hotel on MacDonnell Road, not that I'm there much except for sleeping. Jerry and I work hard and fast, compiling information on twenty-seven acquisition candidates.

One of the junior bankers in the office breaks his foot and I take his place rowing on the company team at the dragon boat races. It's a couple weeks to race day. Daily early-morning practices are a hassle but it feels good to train hard and, thankfully, my sleep deepens.

One morning after practice, I arrive earlier than usual and overhear Jerry on the speakerphone in the conference room.

"Just relax."

Mrs. Worley's voice says, "I can't relax, Jerry."

"You know what happens when you work yourself up — "

Mrs. Worley starts crying.

When Jerry notices me standing in the doorway, he reaches across the table and switches from the speakerphone to the handset. Into the receiver he says, "I'll call you later. No. Lunchtime."

I clear my throat and set my binders on the tabletop.

"Let's get to work, Blank," says Jerry. He leans back in his chair. His eyes are fixed at the line where the ceiling tiles meet the wall.

ॐ ॐ ॐ

We're collating in the conference room when I get a phone call from my old troop mate, RJ. He's been drinking. It's midnight in New Jersey. "Heard you're working in China," he says and I tell him about the temporary transfer to Hong Kong, a little about the project and my changing role.

"Cool," he says and tells me about how his rehabilitation's stalled due to ongoing delays with benefits.

"Jesus Christ."

"I know. They don't care, Blank. They don't fucking care."

"It's a bureaucracy."

RJ is silent awhile and asks, "You still taking Black Rock Hill?"

"You know it," I say and prepare myself for what comes next. It's like a film on TV. RJ can't find the button to turn off the television set and needs me there with him, watching the screen.

"I keep seeing Tony all messed up. Then I'm crawling around in the brush, searching for his arm. Then I wake up," says RJ. His voice is ragged.

I don't respond.

"Promise me you remember that fucking hill, Blank."

"I remember."

We talk for a while longer and then I encourage him to call the benefits service centre first thing in the morning, rattle their chains about his file, and he promises he'll try again.

After I hang up, I wander over to the windows and try not to think about Black Rock Hill. There's no point. It's waiting for me, day and night. The view over the water is obliterated by clouds but I know, across the harbour, the lights of TST burn in the streaming rain.

When I turn back from the windows, Jerry asks, "What the hell happened to you in Afghanistan?"

I consider his broken face. I could change the subject but I don't. "What do you want to know?"

"Anything."

"You never knew when you would be shot at. Snipers from the hilltops could rip your head off at anytime."

"Something happened."

"I'm not going to tell you about it, Jerry."

"I'm a good listener."

"Bullshit."

"All right, I'm a bad listener."

I consider the rain. It never rained in Afghanistan. It was white-hot and dusty and then it snowed. Black-and-white static. I see my hand, too large to be real, buried in Tony's armpit, trying and failing to staunch the flow of his blood. Arteries spurt when they're severed. Never mind.

"You're an anarchist and you don't fucking believe in war, remember?" I say.

"What's that got to do with it?"

"I fucked up, okay?"

"How do you think I ended up in the Hong Kong office? It's a long way from the mothership." Jerry drains his cup of coffee and sets it down with a clatter.

"We were ambushed." This is the simplest way to explain the patrol.

Jerry shifts forward in his chair and holds his large, tanned hands captive on the tabletop. "Tell me about it, Blank."

"Friend of mine died."

"You were there?"

"He was my partner. Of course I was there."

"How'd he die?"

"An RPG ripped his arm off and he bled out."

"Jesus, Blank."

"Jesus had nothing to do with it," I say.

"When did this happen?"

"May 31st, 2004." Almost four years to the day since I fucked up.

☙ ☙ ☙

Early Saturday morning Jerry rings my intercom. "Get up, you bum. Fuck the project. We're going hiking."

When he enters my suite he's carrying a bag of groceries. "Supplies," he says and heads for the kitchen. The kitchen is too small for more than one person. I wedge the swinging door open and stand in the doorway. "I'll make us some big-ass sandwiches," says Jerry. "You got coffee?"

I nod at the freezer.

Jerry brews a pot of coffee and sets to work on the sandwiches.

When the coffee's brewed, I pull cream from the fridge and pour a generous amount into a mug. The coffee's strong and hot and tastes good. "Thanks, Jerry."

"Don't get all touchy-feely on me, soldier." Jerry takes a big gulp of coffee and grimaces from the heat. "Where's the cutting board?"

I reach across the kitchen, pull a rectangle of plastic from the cupboard.

"You're a good guy."

"I'm not a good guy."

"You're a good guy, Blank. I like you and I don't like that many guys." Jerry stops talking for a while. As he washes the dishes he says, "You work hard, you don't complain. And you listen."

"Listening was a big part of my job in the army."

"It's more than basic training, Blank. It's a life skill and it's great for business."

When it's time I place the sandwiches and two big bottles of water into my pack, and slide it onto my back. Outside my building we hail a taxi and head out of the city along the southside. At Shek-O Road, we disembark and start up the stairs at the trailhead.

It's a steep climb through bamboo and woodland forests, deep and lush that tunnel over the trail. The path is full of roots and rocks. When we emerge from the tree line the valleys above are full of brush. I lead the way and Jerry follows. The path is quiet. It's hot. The wind is high and bends the brush in all directions.

The path undulates along the spine of the Dragon's Back and is increasingly rocky. I'm careful where I place my feet. Then a mountain bike shoots past, the rider standing tall in his seat, whooping, wheels jerking on each bounce. He disappears around a corner before I can fully register his presence, then absence.

"Jesus, Blank, I didn't sign up for basic training," says Jerry from behind.

I slow my pace.

At the peak of Shek-O mountain we halt and rest. We eat our sandwiches on a table that doubles as a landmark, coordinates included. Easy to locate. The wind is howling and we cannot speak without shouting. Jerry points out the roof of his house in Big Wave Bay. The view is beautiful. The sea is all around and there are many islands far away in the distance. I think about Tony and wonder if he would've liked Hong Kong. Somehow I doubt it but he never had the chance to find out for himself.

৵৵৵

On Monday morning I poke my head into Mr. Worley's office to ask him about his availability for the first pitch meeting. He's resting his forehead on his desk. I clear my throat several times before he stirs. When he lifts his head, there's an imprint of a binder edge on his cheek.

Without his glasses, his eyes appear larger and his eyelashes are full. His complexion is ashen and there are black smudges under his eyes; he looks like he hasn't slept in a week. He gropes for his glasses without success.

"To the right, sir. Your right."

When Mr. Worley settles his glasses in place I answer his questions about the status of the pitch book.

"Right. Good. I'm counting on you. There's a lot at stake. We've got to get this *exactly* right." Mr. Worley adjusts his cuffs.

His phone rings and he checks the call display and says, "It's head office. I have to take this call. Get out of here, Blank."

❧ ❧ ❧

Right before the road begins its final descent into the village of Stanley, it passes through an avenue of old trees with twisted branches that clutch above the road. Blue sky beyond. Then the road drops rapidly, a thrilling series of curves, and the taxi corners slowly. Apartment complexes climb the hills, vying for the best view over the water. And the sea, a clear light blue, almost turquoise.

A relaxed feeling washes over me and I exhale fully then realize I've been holding my breath. I check my watch. I'm too early for the dragon boat races. I signal the driver to stop and I wander through the market onto the promenade. It's hot. The orange-ringed sun looks funny. There's a weather warning for extreme heat. The seaside is busy. There are small craft crowding the seawall, selling an assortment of fresh fish to the locals.

My cellphone rings.

"Where are you?" asks Jerry, who is offshore on the Morgan Stanley party junk.

"Waiting to row."

"When you're done, you've gotta come out to the party, soldier. I'll introduce you to a couple of my clients." He tells me where to hire a water taxi.

I purchase a bottle of water from a vendor and find a bench to rest in the shade of a palm tree. That's when a man with a facial tumour ambles up and rests on a nearby bench. The tumour is large, the size of a small melon. The skin is discoloured, as if vessels have burst from the pressure. Blood pooling below the surface.

The man is accompanied by his elderly parents who sit on the wall behind him but not before his mother hands him a green hand towel. He holds the towel to his face, covering the growth. One of his eyes is stretched open by the tension of the tumour and cannot close properly. Occasionally he dabs at his weeping eye with the corner of the towel.

The people on the promenade give the man with the tumour a wide berth, cross to the opposite side of the walkway, point and stare. I cannot stop looking and rationalize that he must be accustomed to stares. Still, he sits quietly, even contemplatively, watching people pass. His parents sit with their backs to him.

When a small boy kicks a soccer ball close to his bench, the man with the tumour retrieves it and hands it to the boy. The boy refuses to take the ball and bursts into tears. The boy's parents say something harsh then quickly usher the boy away. The man with the tumour carries the ball back to his bench and rests it gently beside him. Carefully he readjusts his towel. His parents remain seated, with their backs turned.

I stand up too fast and feel dizzy and then I head over to the boat launch to see if any of my teammates have arrived for the race. I join a couple of junior bankers resting in the shade of a flame tree, keeping watch over the company dragon boat.

I lean against the tree trunk, ribbons of red waxy flowers trailing like fresh blood. I close my eyes and let it happen. It has to happen. It's like I'm trapped inside a documentary film. The camera shifts over the grassy field, sunlight glints off Tony's weapons. I gaze down at the grass, flattened by a combination of wind and the bellies of soldiers who've crawled ahead. I taste dirt in my mouth.

There's a buzzing.

"Incoming." My voice sounds muffled.

I scan the environment. There's a line of insurgents below, a line of insurgents above. I panic. I'm running through the field, sucked toward a gnarled black tree, the roar of gunfire in my head. A slumped figure beneath black branches is drawing me closer. Closer, still.

Never mind the blood, the darkening blood. Never mind my hand buried in his gaping armpit. Tony's chalky-blue. He's grimacing and, for some reason, I'm convinced he needs a drink. I give him a sip from my canteen. It's no use. He cannot swallow.

Then Tony points at the barren branches above and says, "The leaves — "

There are no leaves. The tree is burned out.

RJ is scrambling through the brush searching for Tony's arm and, when he locates it, he wraps it in a plastic bag like meat. Carefully he places it at Tony's feet and squats with his back turned, weeping. Waiting for the medevac. I'm holding a pressure dressing and it's no use. Tony's gone missing from his face.

After the medevac departs, I try wiping my hands clean on the trampled grasses. RJ alternates between spitting curses and scrubbing his flak jacket with disposable wipes. There's blood everywhere.

A horn blares and announces another heat. I open my eyes to the orange-ringed sun, the flaming tree, the dragon boats beating across the bay. A marine flare propels into the air and explodes above, a drifting orange light that burns fast and hard and then it's gone. Like Tony. I want to salute but it seems ridiculous to do so, here on a beach on Hong Kong Island.

When the time comes we row several heats until our elimination in the semi-finals. Beaten out by Lehman, again. I arrange for a water taxi to ferry me out to the party junks and prepare myself for mingling with Jerry's clients.

えのえのえの

The party junks are tethered like unruly school children, jostling for a superior view of the dragon boat races. Brightly coloured corporate logos hang from the flagpoles, publicizing the investment banks in Hong Kong.

The day turns overcast and the varnished teak decks of the party junks glow golden beneath imitation paper lanterns. Linked with ropes fore and aft, they are so close that one can hop from one junk to the next. I've heard that as the afternoon progresses, junior bankers jump the circuit, comparing parties.

On the congested deck of the Morgan Stanley I edge through the crowd, search in vain for a seat along the banquet benches. As requested, I introduce myself to Jerry's clients and ensure their drink glasses are full to capacity, try to make small talk.

Lightheaded, I'm overtired from a combination of bursts of rigorous exercise, and the extreme heat and high humidity. Get a grip.

"We lost. What the hell happened?" asks Jerry.

"Just ran out of steam," I say and swallow a bottle of water in one gulp. A waiter carries a loaded tray of drinks past and I grab a green-tinged cocktail. Mojitos. Fresh mint tastes like earth.

"Those rat bastards from Lehman probably cheated."

"Next year." I pluck my sweat dampened T-shirt away from my chest.

"Next year is fucking right." Jerry shakes a fist at Lehman's party junk tied directly to ours. Merrill Lynch is tied beyond Lehman's and Goldman Sachs' farther beyond. Apart from their corporate logos, the party junks are identical, a financial flotilla.

Music skips, scratches.

"Turntables. Jesus. They've got a fucking DJ over there." Jerry squints across at the Lehman party junk, so packed with bankers, clients, and party girls that it sinks down in the water, at least one foot lower than the Morgan Stanley.

"Can you buy turntables anymore?"

"They're obsolete, I'm obsolete. What're they spinning?" Jerry is clad in rumpled shorts and a T-shirt advertising The Clash. He leans against the wooden railing as if he was born on an incline over the South China Sea.

"Sounds like Fall Out Boy."

"Emo shit."

"Pop-punk, actually."

"Oh, and that makes it all right?"

"Punk lives, Jerry."

"Yeah, corporate punk lives. Listen. Gotta check out Lehman's party junk," says Jerry and guzzles low-alcohol beer.

"I'll go." It's well established that senior bankers don't make the party circuit, sending the junior bankers out on reconnaissance. A senior banker found on a competitor's party junk is considered treasonous.

"Nah. Stay put. You're the next Golden Boy," says Jerry and dispatches a couple of sweaty junior bankers loitering on the forward deck. "Whatcha drinking, soldier?"

"Mojitos."

"Minty little fuckers," says Jerry and grimaces.

"Refreshing, actually. Citrusy."

"Don't get your combat shorts in a knot. Where's Worley Man?" Absentmindedly he extracts an elastic from the pocket of his cargo shorts and pushes his unruly hair back into a ponytail.

"The boss is coming?"

Jerry nods. "I wonder if he'll bring Mrs. Worley."

"What's going on with her?"

"Wife number two has clearly defined the enemy lines."

"Speak of the devil," I say and nod.

Mr. Worley makes a beeline for us. As usual he wears a grey suit and highly polished dress shoes. He pointedly ignores me and, instead, starts in on Jerry. "How goes the battle with CRITIC?"

"Yeah, I set up another meeting. Promising, capitalistically speaking." Jerry leans back even further on the wooden railing and braces his tanned, bared feet on the polished deck.

"And?"

"This is not a love song, Worley Man," says Jerry.

Mr. Worley frowns for a split second and says, "You're the Golden Boy, aren't you, Jerry?"

"You want me to pick up a second account."

"Who said anything about a second account?"

"Three accounts can't hurt." Jerry grits his teeth.

"Three accounts would be good," says Mr. Worley and snaps his shirt cuffs down. Then he sails into the crowd, the flaps of his business suit flaring out in a grey wake.

"Three accounts. Jesus. He has no fucking idea. A year sucking up," says Jerry.

"Building relationships." I taste my mojito. Green waves. Sweetness emerges as the dominant flavor. Different with each mouthful.

"Get with the program. You're the next Golden Boy. Listen and learn. A whole year sucking up. To discover they've signed a fucking feng shui with the competitors. A deal no different than yours." Crushing his empty beer can, Jerry chucks it across the water at Lehman's party junk. It bounces off the wooden hull and drops into choppy water.

"Hey. Don't litter," says a young woman from across the narrow margin. She wears a skimpy bikini top and bright-blue board shorts that sit well below her studded umbilicus.

"Barack attacks," says Jerry and points at a campaign button pinned to the brim of her baseball cap.

"You voting for change?" she asks.

"Don't vote," says Jerry. "It's against my principles, politically speaking."

"Apathetic."

"Anarchistic, actually," says Jerry. "Interested?"

She glares at him for a moment and turns away into a cluster of brightly clad party girls. A house beat gathers speed in the background. Gyrating against one another, the girls' arms collectively rise up in a party hallelujah.

"She's feisty, all right. Think I'm in love," says Jerry. He makes a lovestruck face, palm to heart. "Those rat bastards are scratching records and they've got feisty chicks over there. How come our party girls are so boring?"

"They're from credit services."

"True."

"You shouldn't litter."

"It's not like the water's clean, Blank."

"That's not the point."

"Oh, look at you. How old are you, anyway?"

"Twenty-nine." The same age as Jerry was when he made Senior VP. I wonder how a punk like Jerry has managed his career at the bank, with his long hair, loud music, and abrasiveness.

"Twenty-nine. Jesus. I'm too old for this shit," says Jerry and surveys the boat racecourse. "Semi-finals finished?"

I shake my aching head. The wiring's gone to hell.

A squall blows up. Small fishing boats crash across the white-capped bay. Dragon boats leap between buoys and the shouts of the boatmen bounce across the rough, steely water. The beating of the drums intensifies as the dragon boats converge and accelerate toward the finish line.

かかか

Mr. and Mrs. Worley come by a little later. Mrs. Worley's hair is newly cut, short, close to her scalp; the skin on her neck is even paler than her bared shoulders. As she talks, she absentmindedly runs a hand over the fine hairs on her nape.

"How are you?" I ask Mrs. Worley.

"I'm dizzy, Mike," she says and laughs. Then she shows me an intravenous port taped to the back of her trembling hand.

"Canossa Hospital," explains Mr. Worley. His voice is clipped, short as his hair. "She's out on leave for good behaviour."

"I'm trying," she says and stares into the distance. Her hazel eyes are more brown than green and they don't look like they see what she's looking at, but she keeps on looking.

"Trying," says Mr. Worley and anchors his glasses atop the bridge of his nose.

"Don't you want to?" she asks Mr. Worley.

"Who said anything about trying?" says Mr. Worley.

A moment of silence.

"Where's the bar?" asks Mr. Worley.

"I'm not supposed to drink," Mrs. Worley says.

"Who said anything about a drink?" says Mr. Worley, his voice too loud.

He turns to me and asks, "Where's Jerry?"

I point at the forward deck where Jerry dances the limbo in some kind of drinking game, shoulders shimmying. The junk rocks in the wake of passing boats and Jerry collapses in a heap under the horizontal bar, surrounded by a bunch of giggling party girls.

Mrs. Worley laughs. Her chest flushes a pale pink.

"Drinks would definitely be good," says Mr. Worley and disappears in the direction of the bar.

After a moment I ask, "What are you in hospital for?"

"A lobotomy if I'm lucky," she says. "I've been dizzy for the past six months, on and off, and the doc suggested I stay in the hospital. So they could run some tests."

"Did they find anything?"

"Half a brain," says Mrs. Worley and laughs at herself. "It's driving me nuts. The hospital, I mean. Except for the drugs. Legal drugs are better than illegal ones. I see lights where I shouldn't."

"Lucky you."

After a moment she says, "There's this apparatus thingy on the ceiling of my room. I can't figure out what it's for."

"Hanging up medical equipment," I say and tell her about the time I broke my leg. A dirt bike accident resulting in a complicated tibiofibular fracture. Six weeks suspended in traction. I show her my scars.

Mrs. Worley pins me with a stare and says, "You know what it's like. Being confined to hospital."

"I do."

"Come visit me."

I can't think of anything to say.

"C'mon, Mike. We'll make a list. 'Top 10 Reasons We Love Hong Kong'. Doctor's orders," she says. Her pupils are enlarged, ragged, and I wonder exactly what drugs she's on. Avoiding an answer, I flag down a passing waiter, grab a couple mojitos, and down one as quick as I can. Definitely more syrupy than sweet.

Jerry hops down from the forward deck and joins us.

"Like my new hairdo, Jerry?" asks Mrs. Worley and fingers her serrated hair.

"Fucking gorgeous."

"Had to cut it off. The ends broke. Guess I bleached it too many times."

Jerry grins. The sudden warmth in his fractured face soothes my aching head.

"Come and visit me again," she says. "Please?"

Jerry shakes his head.

"You know you want to," she says. She rests her hands, delicate as scallop shells, on Jerry's deeply tanned forearm and leans in. A thin red smear of fresh blood appears under the clear adhesive bandage stabilizing her intravenous port.

"Careful, Mrs. Worley," says Jerry. His face shifts into a shape and doesn't, at the same time. "Have you been drinking?"

"Just one. In the car on the way over," says Mrs. Worley. "You know how parties make me nervous — "

"You promised," Jerry interrupts.

"I'm sorry." Mrs. Worley smoothes down her dress with both hands, as if she's ironing it against her hips.

Jerry is silent.

"You don't know what it's like," she says. "Being the second Mrs. Worley."

Jerry leans toward me and says, "I ever tell you the story of how I found my house?"

"No, sir."

"Had it under surveillance for months from my sailboat. I was living onboard at the time — it's a long story."

"Big Wave Bay is out of this world," says Mrs. Worley. Her voice is overly bright.

"Blazing with lights all night long, every night, a fucking beacon. Nobody coming or going. I couldn't figure it out. Thought I'd try the door and, believe it or not, it was unlocked," says Jerry and lifts his shoulders into a shrug.

"The house was deserted?" asks Mrs. Worley.

Jerry nods.

"You invaded," I say.

"It's appropriation without permission, all right?" says Jerry. "I provide a certain balance, anarchistically speaking."

"You're a bankarchist," I say and realize my head is swimming with minted, syrupy booze. Sore, still.

"Bankarchist! You're all right, Blank. You'll do just fine." Jerry grins so wide his large nose skews to the left, pushing his disjointed features even farther apart. Broken crockery.

"Can you squat in Hong Kong?" asks Mrs. Worley.

"Yeah, me and hundreds of thousands of illegal aliens waiting on the edge of our fucking seats for an eviction notice," says Jerry.

"To reject, anarchistically speaking," I say.

"You got it."

"How long have you lived out there?"

"Three years."

"Any problems?" asks Mrs. Worley.

"A local guy comes around every once in a while asking questions. I tell him I'm subletting."

"He believes you?" I ask.

"I'm a white man living on the post-colonial edge."

"Three years is a long time."

"Tick-tock bangs the clock," says Jerry and pauses for a moment, his electric blue eyes trailing over my face. "When it's all over, you can have it, Blank."

"You're leaving," says Mrs. Worley. She stands still, eyes open wide, staring straight in front of her, moving not a muscle.

At that moment Mr. Worley pushes through the crowd and hands Mrs. Worley a large glass of white wine. His grey suit flaps open exposing snakes-and-ladders stitched suspenders.

"I'll take that, Worley Man," says Jerry and intercepts the wineglass.

Wordlessly Mr. Worley pulls Mrs. Worley away with him.

"You don't get along with Mr. Worley, do you?"

"Who said anything about getting along?" says Jerry.

My laugh sounds muffled. "I've been meaning to ask you. How did you ever end up at Morgan Stanley?"

"Didn't pick the job. The job picked me."

"You like it?"

"I'm a punk, Blank. I took the job as a joke. But I'm good at mergers and acquisitions. It's a fucking curse." Jerry scrubs a hand over his sweating face.

"What's the story with Mrs. Worley, anyway?"

"Cocaine, more cocaine, wine, more wine, even more cocaine, acting out, lotsa cocaine, full blown psychosis. You didn't hear it from me." Jerry pours the contents of Mrs. Worley's glass of wine down his throat and grimaces.

"You were there."

"Yeah, the Golden Boy is always available," says Jerry.

"Hypothetically speaking." I take another sip of my mojito. Now my drink is both cloyingly sweet and overly tangy. Acidic green waves. I fling the plastic drink cup overboard.

"You shouldn't litter," says Jerry quietly.

"Like you said, it's not like the water's clean."

The party junks suddenly crash against one another. I grab the wooden hand railing. Underneath the barrier, my fingers dig into a disintegrating section of the railing; the wood is barely held together with tacky layers of yellow varnish. I brush splinters away.

☘☘☘

As we wait for the final race, the sky darkens and fuses with the sea at the horizon. Rain spits. The junior bankers stationed on the forward deck rush for cover. Someone turns on the fluorescent strip lighting, eradicating the warm glow of fake lanterns. The covered decks of the Morgan Stanley are crowded, humid, and sticky with an afternoon's worth of spilled drinks.

Through the crowd I catch a glimpse of Mrs. Worley. She slumps against a decorated column in the centre of the party junk, Mr. Worley beside her. A strap of her wrinkled cream-coloured dress slides off her pale shoulder.

Blank

Mr. Worley hands her a full glass of white wine and Mrs. Worley sips then cradles her wineglass in her hands. A purple bruise is forming around her blood-smeared bandage, a corner of the adhesive lifts and her intravenous port droops.

Jerry looks like he wants to say something and changes his mind. Something surfaces in the lines and fractures of his face, fierce, lonely, and regretful. I picture Jerry alone in his beautiful house overlooking the rough surf of Big Wave Bay. An earthy humidity sticks in my throat.

"I'm crossing over," says Jerry and takes a flying leap across the watery divide, landing squarely on the Lehman party junk. After he's gained his footing, he turns back and throws his house keys at me, and shouts good luck. When he gives a half-assed salute, I shake my fist in his direction.

LEON

AN IMMENSE BLACK-AND-WHITE billboard of a near-naked man hovers in the polluted haze. Over twenty stories high, the gigantic man leans, his head tilted back, against the soon-to-be-demolished Ritz-Carleton Hotel. His eyes are almost entirely closed. Tight white underpants contrast glistening black skin.

Leon finds he cannot sleep. Not that The Giant is staring, exactly; his eyes are barely discernible. Still, a vague feeling that The Giant is watching lingers in Leon's consciousness, a feeling that, somehow, images are radiating onto The Giant's retinas. Not that Leon has enough time to sleep these days; he's spending most of his time at work implementing the latest risk management system, a relatively simple install that isn't anywhere near finished.

It's probably just as well that the project isn't complete because then Leon would have to explain how it works and he doesn't fully understand hedging risk with derivatives. Leon regularly pulls out the complex and tangential flowchart he created, graphics included, and tracks his demise from the bank; he estimates he's somewhere near the halfway point. At this rate, it will take a miracle to implement the system and, when Leon announces the inevitable delay, he'll be placed on probation. What's more, when he admits his inability to comprehend risk management, it'll be gore on granite: his chopped head rolling down the marble hallways of the bank.

His cellphone rings.

"It's Thursday," says Load Toad, an Englishman Leon met in a bar not long after he landed. A thirsty Englishman with extensive experience, business and otherwise, both in Hong Kong and Mainland China.

"My project," says Leon.

"Your bloody project," says Load Toad. "See you at the pub. Decker's waiting."

Leon clicks off his computer and mentally shifts himself over to the "Thursday Night" feedback loop on his flowchart. At the pub, Leon pushes his way through the crowd to the usual spot, already littered with Load Toad's orderly line of pint glasses, an overflowing ashtray, and Decker's many cellphones. Idiosyncrasies, thinks Leon then remembers his flowchart. Empties, electronics, and the Thursday Night feedback loop: the three dimensions of his social life in Hong Kong.

"Iced cold lager?" asks Load Toad.

"Or three," says Leon.

"Sorted." Load Toad waves down the bartender.

"Fucking iPod died," says Decker and slides the cobalt blue unit into his shirt pocket.

"What are you listening to?"

"Some new Manchester band Load Toad told me about," says Decker.

"Any good?"

"Dunno yet."

"Manc music," says Load Toad and tidies his pint glasses into a new improved line. "I ever tell you about the time I saw Joy Division at the Factory Club?" He launches into his *Manc-Music-is-Fucking-Brilliant* speech; Leon estimates it should run seventeen minutes, give or take, and presses the stopwatch function on his new dive wristwatch.

"The Giant is getting on my nerves," he interrupts at the fourteen-minute mark. Another round slides across the bar.

"The Rude Giant on the Ritz-Carlton?" asks Load Toad, mid-sentence.

Leon nods.

"Helluva package The Giant's carrying," says Decker. "Semi-erect, his cock must be two stories high. He's giving me a complex, if you know what I mean. Loady, what's Viagra like?"

"Bastard. The Giant's a young'un and shouldn't need supplements," says Load Toad, pudgy fingers tugging on his shaggy sideburns.

"The Giant's seriously ripped," says Leon. "Must work out."

"You gym rats. Always sizing each other up. You light in the loafers, Leon?" asks Load Toad. "Not that there's anything wrong with that."

"I go to the gym on a regular basis; doesn't make me a gym rat or a homosexual," says Leon and realizes he's missed his daily workout twice this week. Too tired.

"Yeah, Leon's a metro sexual," says Decker and deftly rolls his sleeves above his elbows. A red-and-blue fishtail flickers out beneath his cuff. "Like my new shirt, Leon? I think I'm gonna score."

"It's striped," says Leon. All of Decker's shirts are striped. Not that it matters. Decker attracts women without trying.

"Why mess with a sure thing?" asks Decker, tapping a cigarette loose from a crumpled pack of Marlboros. *Veni, vidi, vici.* Almost perfect for Decker, thinks Leon. Should be *I came, I saw, I came.*

"How'd they get the billboard up on the building, anyhow?" asks Leon. The bartender hops up onto the counter behind the bar and pulls down bottles the colour of a tropical sky.

"Dunno. Dropped it down the side? Looks like canvas. It ripples when the wind comes up," says Decker and strikes a stylized Zippo lighter; extraterrestrial eyes bugging out of stainless steel.

"The exotic eastern wind. That explains The Giant's erection," says Load Toad, grinning.

"There've been civic complaints," says Leon and checks his messages. Nothing urgent, just a couple of inane questions from his team, who are all still at work.

"Fuck indecency," says Decker, exhaling roughly. His face is veiled with cigarette smoke. "They're just pissed The Giant's black. Hong Kongers don't embrace darker skinned races, if you know what I mean."

"I know what you mean, Decker," says Leon. He's second generation Canadian, a mix of Caucasian and East Indian. Twelve months in Hong Kong have taught him that being studiously ignored at the lunch counter is nothing.

"Don't embrace Caucasians, either. The Eurasian side of the family aren't invited to Sunday dim sum," says Load Toad.

"Could be worse. My ex-wife was accused of prostitution almost every time she came through airport immigration," says Decker.

"Racialist bastards," says Load Toad and shakes his head.

"You were married?" Leon asks Decker.

"Yeah, six years."

"How's she doing?" asks Load Toad.

"Good, good. Business is bustling. She owns a couple high-end boutiques in Kuala Lumpur," Decker says in Leon's direction.

"First-rate, that one," says Load Toad.

"Damn straight." Decker stalks off.

"What happened?" asks Leon.

"Don't ask," says Load Toad.

"Heard about a new bar. Probably posh enough for a *metro sexual* such as yourself," Load Toad says to Leon when Decker returns with another round. Eventually they walk down to Lan Kwai Fong to a bar with no permanent signage, just a glowing purple symbol.

"What is it?" asks Decker.

"A mutant onion," says Load Toad.

"A sign that I'm done for if I don't finish this project," says Leon and kicks at broken pavement.

"Quit complaining, the project will get done," says Decker, pulling out a cellphone to take a picture of the sign. "Shit. Phone's dead." He gropes his pockets for another. Decker's compulsion for sharing images with his friends via email is neverending. The theme, however, changes. Thank God he's through the *what-I-ate-for-dinner* focus, thinks Leon.

"I think it's Morse code for trouble," says Load Toad. "Speaking of trouble, I better call the wife. Let her know I'm running a wee bit late."

"Yeah, I'm pretty sure she knows," says Decker, flicking his cigarette into the street. They dive into the tiny packed bar, a dark blue heaven, house music throbbing. Somehow Decker scores a minuscule table on the edge of the patio, with a direct view down the crowded pedestrian street. Neon signs stack above open doorways.

"Table's the size of a postage stamp," says Load Toad and flags down the waitress, grilling her regarding English beers on tap. She shrugs no, lifts her hair off her neck, and smiles, exposing a crooked overbite.

"No Beamish, are they bloody crazy," says Load Toad.

"How about Red Bull and vodka?" asks Leon.

"I can't drink that caffeinated shit," says Decker. "How about JD?"

Jack Daniel's. Leon compartmentalizes the two words and mentally adds another box labelled "Recover from Massive Hangover" to his "Thursday Night" feedback loop.

Substandard beverage orders are placed and the waitress departs. "I'm a sucker for an overbite," sighs Decker as they watch her hustle back to the bar.

"It's fetching," says Load Toad.

"Her ass or her overbite?" asks Leon.

"Both, actually, ta."

"I ever tell you about my one and only Red Bull and vodka session?" asks Decker a little later. "Drank so much I was fucking vibrating. Heart palpitations too. Drove out to Sai Kung at five in the morning, shirtless, with the top down on the Beamer, trying to cool off. Stayed up thirty-six hours."

"Christ," says Load Toad. "That's a record."

"Epic feedback loop," says Leon and beats the rhythm of the music onto his knees.

"You and your fucking flowcharts," Decker says to Leon.

"You and your fucking phones," Load Toad says to Decker.

"You and your fucking empties," says Leon and points at Load Toad's stack of highball glasses.

They talk business and girls, not necessarily in that order. Load Toad's worried about his suppliers coming through with the next shipment of pigments by September; Decker's concerned about another major reorganization at work; and, Leon's head is about to be chopped for being a fake, a phony, a *risk imposter*. Thank God for Thursday nights, he thinks and checks again for messages.

"Give me that," says Load Toad and disappears Leon's Blackberry.

"Babes, three o'clock," Decker says under his breath and nods at a group of young expatriate women settling into an adjoining table.

Load Toad leans over and says, "What d'you ladies think of The Rude Giant?"

Blank stares.

"The billboard on the Ritz-Carleton," says Decker.

"He's gorgeous," says a woman and sweeps wispy bangs aside. Her eyes are contained in black kohl.

"According to *Leon*, The Giant's ripped," says Load Toad.

"I keep dreaming about him," says another woman, a little older than the rest, a polka-dot scarf draped across her shoulders.

"Yeah, you'll need a smoke," Decker says and pulls out a fresh pack of Marlboros: a white peak dominates red cellophane sky. Like Caucasians in Hong Kong, thinks Leon and stabs at his ice cubes with a stirstick.

Ribald laughter.

"It's a sexualized image of a man, which is pretty surprising in this city, don't you think," says the kohl-eyed woman to Leon. "It's usually the other way round."

"He's getting on my nerves," says Leon.

"You said that," says Decker.

"Why?" asks Load Toad, pursing his fleshy lips.

"I think he's watching me," Leon says.

"Maybe The Giant has x-ray vision. Sees through people and such," says Load Toad after a moment.

"Lucky man. He can see everyone naked," says Decker and grins.

"If you have enough money in this city, you can see anyone naked, eh, Decker? No. The Giant is closing his eyes so he can't see the scary stuff," says Load Toad.

"You think so," says Leon.

"He'd see all kinds. Like whatever's buried in alleyways. Makes me think of the Walled City in Kowloon. All kinds of bits and pieces hidden in there. Human remains, probably," says Load Toad.

"Yeah," says Decker and sniffs like there's a whiff of wet garbage stuck in his nose.

"What's the Walled City?" asks the kohl-eyed woman.

"A squat made up of several buildings, cobbled together with bamboo scaffolding, electrical cords. A living creature, it was.

Thirty thousand people living on top of one another. Demolished now, thank Christ," says Load Toad.

"Didn't some journalist take a bunch of photographs before the wrecking ball hit?" asks Decker.

"Put out a coffee-table book," says Load Toad.

"A coffee-table book about a squat," says Leon.

"It's true," says Load Toad and shrugs his shoulders like they're too heavy.

"If you package it, you can sell anything," says the kohl-eyed woman.

"You ever go in the Walled City, Loady?" asks Decker.

"Nah. Story is the *police* didn't go in there. You'd be killed. Not that anybody belongs," says Load Toad and re-stacks his empties into a glassy arc.

And Leon recalls an encounter a few months earlier with an old Chinese shopkeeper wearing a monochromatic Mao suit who, brandishing a dirty broom worn down to a forty-five-degree angle, thwacked his leg. He was walking past her household goods shop when she hit him for no apparent reason. Broke his skin.

"I can't sleep," he says, to no one in particular.

"Just ignore Leon. Problems at work. He *promises* not to go on about it," says Load Toad.

"What do you do?" The kohl-eyed woman crosses her legs. As her skirt falls away Leon can't help following the line of her thigh, pausing on her triangular kneecap.

"Work at a bank," he says.

"Ask him to show you his flowchart," says Load Toad and flags down the waitress. "*Very* sexy."

"Flowcharts can be sexy," she says. In the humidity, her eyeliner is smudged and Leon fights the urge to reach over and smooth it out with his fingertip.

"Speaking of sexy, do you like my new shirt?" asks Decker.

"It's striped," she says.

Leon laughs.

More drinks arrive at the now-conjoined tables. They laugh at Load Toad's stories about factory trips into Guangdong Province, the mix-ups and mistakes. A street vendor wanders up, hawking glow-in-the-dark sticks across imaginary patio walls before the bouncer forces him to move along. "Neon chromosomes," says Leon without thinking and that's when he realizes he's drunk.

"I glow in the dark," the kohl-eyed woman whispers in his ear. Leon's attention narrows into a point on her bare shoulder and he thinks she's probably right. Her skin is remarkably pale.

Somehow she drags Load Toad, protesting, up onto the crowded dance floor. Leon catches a glimpse of him a little while later, caught in a blue dot, swaying, his arms outstretched like Christ the Redeemer. When Load Toad eventually comes back to the table, he leans on Leon and says, "She likes you."

"The Giant is killing my mojo," complains Decker and shoves at his shirt sleeves like they're tourniquets.

ৰু ৰু ৰু

"MacDonnell doh," she says to the taxi driver. Her Cantonese is brutal. The driver mutters under his breath and they're afloat in a sea of pulsing brake lights. As they surge around a complicated overpass, she kisses Leon, throwing them off balance into the backseat corner. The driver grumbles louder and turns up the radio.

Her building, shrouded in a green, plastic tarp that wrinkles around the entranceway, is laced up with bamboo scaffolding. "Renovations," she says and shrugs. Leon thinks she looks appealing in her sleeveless dress, shoes dangling from one hand. As the lift ascends, the shuttered eye of a security camera whirs and clicks. Reflexively he smoothes down his hair.

She kisses him again.

Fourteenth floor, turn left at the lift, thinks Leon. Reverse the process on the way out. A quick glance around her studio flat reveals that it's almost empty. No curtains adorn the windows. A pile of moving boxes slumps into one corner next to an unmade bed.

She slips out of her dress and poses before exposed plate glass. The tarp skin casts a green glow through the windows. Crossing her arms over her breasts she turns, exposing the knuckles of her spine. Another line, thinks Leon and slides forward, joining her. When she pulls his clothes away she says, "You're very fit."

"I work out," says Leon. His words catch in his throat when he realizes that The Giant has a clear view and worries aloud that he will spy on them having sex.

"Let him watch," she says, staring down at The Giant. "I bet he thinks he's fucking magnificent." Her tone is abrupt like the Cantonese she spoke to the taxi driver earlier. Then she asks Leon to wear a strap-on dildo that she extracts from a packing box.

"But I have one," he says and gestures.

She insists and demands, "Tie me to the window."

He doesn't want to do it but does it anyway. Tying her wrists to the safety bars is easy. The leather strap of the dildo cuts into his hip almost immediately and he has difficulty finding the correct angle. My rhythm is off, he thinks and shifts position.

"I think I'll go," he says after a while.

"You think you'll go. Dumb fuck." Her eyes are bleeding kohl.

"Don't say that," says Leon.

"I can say whatever I want," she says and stares up at him like dirty glass underfoot. He thinks of the old Chinese shopkeeper with her sharp-edged broom. Straw scraping skin. An isolated unit of Leon slips across a boundary and he screws her until a groan of pleasure slides from her lips. He dresses and leaves her there, sexually aroused, one wrist tied to the safety bars.

At the doorway, Leon turns back. She's unravelling a silk scarf. The air fills with an unfamiliar, continuous light and her naked skin starts glowing greenish-blue. He wonders if it's financial data streaming up from the banks below, merging with neon molecules, creating up-to-the-minute computer code. Like a futuristic capital, thinks Leon. A city of shopkeepers, below, and a city of information, above.

Merrilou

MERRILOU SET THE ironing board beneath the dining room window. Outside, a steady rain blurred the horizon of the South China Sea. The room was dim. Across Stanley Village Road, the floodlights on the grounds of The Crest reflected across the deserted swimming pool, and Merrilou wondered if she would ever leave this city. This morning her son had called, asking for money for another dress. She'd already sent him money for a frothy pale-pink gown with a sweetheart neckline.

Merrilou paused to refill the iron with water. The Mrs. had a heavy iron, a perfect weight. She started in on a linen shirt the colour of coral and the *tamp tamp tamp* of the iron soothed. Money for another dress. Merrilou was a bank for her son. She struggled with this on a weekly basis — money orders from Mami.

The iron hissed and she smelled rust in the vapours; the pipes in the flat weren't clean. She should've filled the iron with bottled water from the dispenser in the kitchen. She should've. Merrilou was a bank for her son. She knew it was her fault and there was no one to blame — she'd left him with her mother when he was ten months old. When she'd signed her first contract as a live-in domestic in Hong Kong.

"It's so beautiful," he'd said.

"I just sent money for the rice."

"But it's graduation." He'd continued for several minutes, describing the dress in detail, and she had to admit it sounded lovely. Mermaid style with a corseted bodice. She could picture him wearing it; he looked attractive in red, more crimson than blood.

"It needs beads on the bodice. Can I send to you?"

"I have no time. I'm working."

"But it's your talent, Mami." And he'd first complimented then pleaded until she'd stopped speaking. Merrilou took pleasure in handwork and her sewing was well regarded in her neighbourhood in Manila. Somehow, by the end of the call, she'd agreed to teach him the art of appliqué and beading on her next home visit.

Merrilou loved ironing. It was predictable. After spraying starch from an aerosol can then flicking water drops onto the light fabric, she pressed the iron down hard. Another short burst of steam and she slid a pair of khaki pants onto a hanger, and hooked them over the curtain rod. Wind thrashed rain-splattered leaves against glass. She considered cracking the window open for fresh air but the moisture would ruin the freshly pressed clothes.

Where would she come up with money for another dress? Could she take another part-time job like this one? Merrilou was lucky to have an understanding employer who allowed her to moonlight, as long as she finished her work first. He insisted on a different neighbourhood, the farther away from Sai Kung, the better. People gossip. Moonlighting was illegal and she had to be careful because, if discovered by Immigration, she would be deported. No. When Merrilou took an ironing job she was selective — professional expatriate couples were the best because, between work and travel, they were rarely home. She could iron in peace. Part-time work made a big financial difference.

After she finished and cleared up her supplies, she locked the flat and walked to the bus stop. It had stopped raining. A man in a green sports car pulled to an abrupt halt, leaned across the passenger seat and asked, "Care for a ride into the city?" He was wearing a polo shirt and a Cartier watch with bead-like jewels on the face. His hands were manicured, tanned fingers tapped the leather-clad steering wheel.

Merrilou knew what this question meant. It was something she'd occasionally done before. Sat alone in expat bars and waited for a man to ask her to accompany him home for the night. Sometimes it was for money and other times, for company.

The bus pulled in behind the sports car and honked.

She searched the man's face and said, "No, thank you." He shrugged like he didn't care one way or the other, waved an attractive hand in her direction, and accelerated toward the traffic circle.

The bus hissed to a stop.

"Why you talk to that man?" asked the bus driver and jerked his head at the sports car. His uniform was too tight and a roll of fat spilled over his dull-white collar — the shirt needed bleaching.

"It's none of your business what I am doing," said Merrilou and immediately regretted talking back. She couldn't risk drawing attention to herself. What if the driver reported her to Immigration?

"Dark devil. Going with men."

"Excuse me?"

"Get in, get in." The driver's eyes were angry, flat.

"I will wait for the next bus."

"Stupid." The driver snapped the door lever shut.

Instead of waiting, Merrilou walked into Stanley along the beach road. Past the octagon-shaped building with the over-sized American flag and around the corner, down the steep hill and alongside the empty main beach. Curtains of seawater slapped against the sand and she ran along the edge as if she were being chased, escaping the foaming water at the last moment. Her bared feet gouged footprints from the coarse sand before the next wave erased all evidence.

It was late by the time she reached her employer's house, the aroma of garlic and chili lingered in the kitchen. The cook, a retired Gurkha, had a talent for all kinds of food, particularly Thai curry, one of her favourites. Merrilou ate standing at the sink. In the dark, she undressed and carefully hung her Tencel skirt from Marks & Spencer in the small wardrobe. Her room, with its barred windows opened wide, smelled of rain and spray starch.

MARK

THE AMERICAN CLUB: a peach building that clings to the rocky shores. Mark wanders out to the poolside after his morning workout. Sunlight explodes off the deck in every direction and momentarily blinds him. He pats his pockets. Useless. His sunglasses are in the car, melting into the dashboard.

On the pool deck, expatriate women huddle over coffee cups, chat about maid troubles and difficulties obtaining airline tickets for their next home visit. The women dab at their upper lips and fan themselves. Their eavesdropping children alternate between paddling in the kiddie pool and hanging their tanned feet above the deep water pool. Waiting for the all-clear.

Off to one side sits a handsome woman in a blue bikini, suntanning. She hooks a finger through the nosepiece of her designer sunglasses, slides them down the long edge of her nose, and gives him the once over. Emerald green irises contrast sharp against the whites of her eyes.

"Hey, you're new," calls the woman and waves him over. "Where're you living?"

"Stanley."

"What complex?"

After a couple of months, Mark isn't accustomed to Hong Kongers and their preoccupation with exactly which building you live in, right down to the unit. "Stanley Court," he says and cheats her out of his house number.

She lifts one eyebrow. "Not bad, neighbour. Where are you from?"

"Canada."

"A polite Canadian. Where's your wife?"

"At work." Debra, the dutiful daughter, is busy growing her father's media empire.

"Kids?"

"Not yet."

"Me, neither." Emerald-tinted eyes disappear behind sunglasses.

The boys skitter across the pool, one after the other, stiff arms flashing. They must have received the go-ahead to enter deeper water. When will Debra send him a sign that it's time to start a family? This question is followed by another that he's been ignoring the last couple of months, about whether Debra really wants kids. She keeps putting off their appointment with the fertility clinic, insisting on letting nature take its course.

"Let's have a drink," says the woman. "I'm Mona, by the way."

"Mark," he says. "Uh. It's ten-thirty in the morning."

"C'mon. You're not a prude, are you?"

Mark shakes his head and perches on an adjoining sun lounger. Does he look like a tightass? Maybe it's the chinos. He's self-scheduled to head back and check his investments, secure a few trades, make $500 US, and call it a day.

"It's twelve o'clock somewhere," says Mona. She waggle-waves her half-full glass and something citrusy that smells like gin sloshes onto her tanned thighs. "I'll have another," she informs the waiter. "And the Canuck will have a scotch-scotch."

"A what?" asks Mark.

"A double scotch. Don't worry. He understands my language."

The morning crosses over to afternoon and they shift under the shade of the umbrella. Mona's a talker. She tells stories about the people she's met, the characters, the big shots and losers. "We're here for a couple years," she says. "And then, who knows?"

Mona drops her slender frame into the water and swims laps with brisk, firm strokes. Her turns are flawless. She darts to one side and surfaces in the middle of the boy pod. She balances a boy on cradled hands then tosses him up and over. The boys clamour for her attention. One after the other, their slippery brown bodies fly through the air and crash into the water. The harder, the better.

The boys' shrieks splash clean across the pool deck. It isn't long before their mothers' frowns stick, before they haul their suntan oil-slicked boys out by the armpits and wrap them in towels as tight as straightjackets.

"C'mon, you know how boys are. They're having fun," says Mona.

"Too much fun," says one mother. "Like someone else we know."

"Shove another coconut tart in your fat mouth, will you?" says Mona.

"Bitch," says another mother.

Mona pushes off the wall into the backstroke, her broad shoulders rushing through the water. A frothy, V-shaped wake dashes against green tiles. Her thick, gold necklace glints in the sunlight, the ornate cross caught in the straps of her bikini.

Mark

The boys slump against one another, throw pleading stares across the pool at Mark as if he has something to do with their freedom. The waiters huddle in the shade around the bar. Mark catches a whiff of something that reminds him of the fruit market at the end of a hot summer day.

"Canuck," calls Mona from the deep end.

Mark approaches the poolside on unsteady legs. Shouldn't have had the third scotch-scotch. As he squats, she clutches his ankle, pulls him off balance and he's underwater before he knows it. Thrashing, he kicks his shoes off and watches them sink to the bottom before he surfaces.

Mark's eyelashes stick together as if he's waking from a jet-lagged sleep. Up close and grinning, she circles and straddles him. "Might as well give them something to talk about," she whispers and nibbles at his earlobe a moment before biting down.

"What the hell?" Mark jerks away. Scrabbling to the wall, he drags himself to a standing position on the pool deck. Once upright, he checks his earlobe for blood. He sways then abruptly coughs up phlegm, thick with the vomit of scotch and it spews onto the flowering shrubs.

"That's disgusting," says a voice from the motherland.

A little boy smirks and gives him the thumbs up. Mark fights the urge to grin back. Instead he says, "Don't spit," in the little boys' direction and strides off toward the locker rooms.

"You okay, Canuck?"

Mark ignores her.

૨⊱ ૨⊱ ૨⊱

The next morning, he finds his water-stained loafers neatly lined up on his doorstep and chucks them in the dumpster. Slamming the lid, he dislodges several trash bags that rest against the bin. Rats scurry away with naked tails dragging.

"You run, don't you?" calls one of his neighbours from the parking lot. Leaning against a dented silver Jaguar, the man absentmindedly traces the empty space where the hood ornament used to be.

Mark nods and tries to remember the man's first name. Perry?

"I'm with the Hash Harriers. A gentleman's running club, good fun. We're racing tonight. Care to join?"

Mark stares at his neighbour's peeling forehead. The evening stretches. Three hours of English programming on television, BBC nature documentaries. Mindless online scrolling. He agrees then waves his neighbour off to work, still trying to remember his name.

That evening, he hooks up with Gary-not-Perry and the rest of the running club at the gas station in Black's Link. The club numbers thirty, young and old, who smile cautiously as they shake hands, clap one another on the shoulders. A variety of accents mingle — Brits, Americans, Scandinavians, and Eastern Bloc. Mark wipes his palms before a rally of handshakes and introductions he's certain to forget.

"Who're you here with?" asks a lanky American wearing a faded blue T-shirt.

"No one. I mean, I invest. My wife works — "

"An independent businessman," says Gary-not-Perry quickly. He launches into a convoluted explanation of Hash terminology. "The FRB is the Front-Running Bastard. He finds the checks and guides the Hounds along. I don't think we're off the pathways. One never knows."

The Hounds stand in a circle. Mark should stretch or do some knee-raises to prepare for the run but no one's moving. No one's talking either. Instead Mark adjusts the shoelaces of his new Adidas runners.

"You need a hashtag. How about cockroach?" says Gary-not-Perry.

"Cockroach, cockroach," shout the Hounds and they raise their hands above their heads. The American reaches over and gives Mark a little shot on the arm.

Without warning the FRB calls the run and sprints down the trail past the Pagoda, churning up gravel. The Hounds force themselves into a pack and drag Mark along like a gangly pup wearing a tight collar.

"Are you," shout the Hounds.

An independent businessman?

"Checking," the FRB shouts back.

The Hounds race down the steep mountain path, run-stumbling, flashing empty smiles at one another. It's all about moving forward, trying to stay upright, and Mark can barely keep his body under control. It's frightening and exhilarating at the same time. When the American shoves past, Mark trips over a rock and launches into the bushes.

The Hounds run on.

Mark stares up at the sky. The treetops frame a blue-sky bowl. Clouds lace themselves together, again and again. Leaves rustle in the wind. Mark tries to imagine himself inside the wind, as if it could carry him someplace else, someplace familiar. A cream-and-black butterfly drifts down. It lands next to him and opens, exposing red splatters along the edges of its wings — inky spikes, marking tremors.

Another butterfly falters and comes in for a landing. And another, and another, and yet another. Before long wings twitch all around him, the insects waiting for a sign. None appears. One by one, they slide off waxy leaves and fall to the ground like smoldering embers. As they die, their wings fold together, exposing soft, grey undersides.

He's lost. He's not carrying any identification and can't think where his papers are located in the flat, exactly. Would anyone notice his absence? Debra's in Singapore on business, something to do with another acquisition.

In the distance the Hounds shout "cockroach". Somehow he extricates himself from the bushes, chases after them. Branches whip him. Prickly bushes grab at him, scratch his arms and legs, drawing blood. A wretched humidity presses down and sweat courses through his hair. He stops in a small clearing and listens. Silence except for ragged breathing.

"On-on," calls the FRB in the near distance.

Breaking through several walls of shrubs and flowering hibiscus, Mark skids to a halt at the front of the pack. The FRB kneels in the scree, pushes aside rocky debris, searching. An indistinct mark emerges, more like a smudge. It's a false sign.

"You're useless. Fuck-ing useless," the American says to the FRB.

The Hounds return to the original check, the American harassing the FRB the entire way, while the Hounds laugh with a mixture of derision and agreement. In response the FRB picks up the pace.

Mark struggles to stay with the pack but eventually leaves a couple men trailing behind. "All this for a couple beers," he hears one grumble. "Chinese or Indian tonight?" asks the other.

Their muffled debate fades. Soon the pace slows and Mark gains control of his breathing, forcing it into rhythm with his steps. In, out. Kids, no kids. Sweat burns his eyes.

❧ ❧ ❧

"How was the run?" asks Debra before he's able to tell her about it.

"How did you know about the run?"

"I asked Gary to keep an eye on you."

"How would you like it if I asked somebody to keep an eye on you?" Mark dares her to speak and, predictably, she's silent. For someone who manages extensive media holdings, she doesn't really communicate.

"How's Singapore?" he asks.

"Sunny and hot."

"Where're you staying?"

"The Grand Hyatt. Listen, I've gotta run. Dad's waiting."

❧ ❧ ❧

Mark ditches the car at the Tai Tam reservoir and runs back toward Stanley, taking it easy on the hills. He barely manages it, his knees aching from the Hash run. With relief, he clears the congested entrances to the market and the bus barns then heads uphill along Wong Ma Kok Road. A salty sea breeze pushes him alongside the college playing fields, as if he was pollen, weightless.

The sound of footfalls approaching from behind and a familiar blonde head emerges. "Mind if I join you?" asks Mona and falls in stride.

They run in silence to the garbage processing plant, turn around and head back the way they came. She pulls him to a stop at the base of the staircase that leads to the Military Cemetery. "Let's take a look. There's a bunch of Canucks buried here."

Mark slowly climbs the steep white stairs, Mona trailing. When they reach the uppermost landing, he turns back and surveys the view over St. Stephen's Beach, empty except for unruly trash piles between BBQ pits. The tide is out, exposing slippery rocks covered with barnacles. A kayak track marks the glistening sand, the abandoned craft tipped on its side against a lifeguard tower. In the distance Mark spies the ferry fast approaching the jetty, and a few lucky cars weighed down with colourful surfboards, awaiting passage to the outlying islands.

"Your legs are scratched. What happened?" asks Mona. He tells her about the mechanics of a Hash run and how he ended up lost in the bushes in Black's Link. "You can't get lost on this island," says Mona. "Believe me, I've tried."

Wandering through the cemetery, they examine row upon row of white headstones. The markers stare out onto an empty turf stage. Beyond lies a barbed wire fence that barely restrains a wild hedge. Further beyond are the college grounds, once used as an internment camp by the Japanese.

They stroll along the narrow terraces, picking out Canadians. Kelly, Fairley, Melville and Sheldon. Damant and Sharp, too. Collectively gathered in a grave. Crowded together and no visitors. Like living in Hong Kong. Mark jumps down to the next level.

"Read an article in the paper about the Canucks. Slaughtered in the battle of Hong Kong. Poor guys." Mona hops down beside him and pats a headstone. "The city surrendered on Christmas Day. Not much of a Christmas, was it, MacFarlane?" she asks the gravestone. "You Canucks are all Scottish, aren't you?"

"Not all."

"What's is all aboot, MacFarlane," she asks the headstone. Her Brooklyn accent draws the 'ooo' out into an 'aaa' and Mark laughs.

Mona pokes him in the ribs, he pushes her back, and she turns over her ankle. When she tries to avoid stepping directly on MacFarlane's final resting place, he grabs for her and they fall onto sparse, prickly grass. She, sprawled in front of the gravestone. He, halfway across her. They, on top of MacFarlane.

She kisses him and he tastes gin. He finds himself kissing. His tongue teases her lips open a little, retreats, then slides along the edge of her teeth. Something changes. Mona twists her tongue into his mouth. Excited by her sharp, grainy flavour, his eyelids sink shut on their own.

Long, slow kisses. He hardens, nosing up and out of the waistband of his running shorts. She fingers the tip until he's moist and his moans echo around the amphitheatre of graves. Mark wonders if they have an audience from the terraces above. He doesn't care. His pelvis aches for elliptical movement. More than anything he craves forgetting what he's become — a househusband.

Mona cries out when he unexpectedly comes across her flat belly. When he's able to open his eyes, he notices that hers are teary and bloodshot.

"It's such a fucking waste." She blots the wet stain with the tail of his T-shirt.

"A waste?"

"I can't have kids. I mean. The doctor says I can't get pregnant."

"Me neither." Mark forces himself to sit up, fights to slow his breath.

"Well, *of course* you can't get pregnant." Mona laughs.

"My wife. I mean, my wife."

"Her too?"

"No, not that."

"I know what you mean." Her voice empties out.

They sit in silence in the cemetery until the groundskeeper arrives with a lawnmower.

ॐ ॐ ॐ

Mark surveys the battered shore. Yellow hazard tape circles Stanley's main beach and a large sign announces that improvement works are in progress. The beach is closed. Sanitation workers have excavated down several feet, trucking the sand away to a processing plant. They're combing out biomedical waste, the used hypodermic needles and other health paraphernalia that wash ashore. Cleaning out chemicals that saturate the sand, pesticides sprayed on the roads each week that, during heavy rains, run onto the beach and into the sea.

A sanitation worker approaches and points at the sign.

Mark shrugs and sits beneath a flaming tree.

"Stupid," says the workman and stalks away.

Mark watches Mona pull off her sundress. Her bikini top folds where fuller breasts previously existed, her ribs flare out like wings. She drops her gauzy clothing onto the wet sand and gallops into the deep sandy pit where the beach used to be.

She hurtles through waves and strikes out for deeper water, diving and rolling like one of the little boys at the American Club pool on the first day. He tries not to watch and, instead, goes through a series of stretches. It isn't long before he's searching the gold-tipped waves.

Mark

There. Rising out of the surf, her water-darkened hair is loosely braided with salt and clings to her neck. She plucks at shredded plastic bags floating in front of her, turns and flings the synthetic weeds out to sea. As the fiery sun slips down the horizon closer to home, Mark thinks about the bloodstained butterflies falling onto the forest floor.

The Suitable Dress

SARAH WAKES TO heavy rain. Without thinking, she rushes to the windows and checks that they're closed and locked. Staring out into a black-tinged cloud, she realizes the skyline of Hong Kong has gone missing and she's in dangerous territory. Shouldn't have signed a sublet sight unseen, she thinks, and hustles back to relative safety.

Three months earlier, Sarah moved in directly from the airport and woke lightheaded. Thought the dizzy episodes were jet lag until they worsened and she vomited whenever she neared the floor-to-ceiling windows. After a trip to the clinic, a diagnosis of acrophobia materialized. Vertigo was the primary symptom. The doctor offered her anti-anxiety tablets.

"I'm not anxious," said Sarah. "I'm dizzy."

The doctor shrugged and handed her a prescription.

Sarah discovered she could manage if she remained on the inside half of the flat, closest to the metal spine of the elevator shaft. It was difficult to stay away from the windows; the neon vista inexplicably pulled her forward. Through trial and error, she defined a boundary. Purchased a large roll of silver duct tape and laid down the vertigo line.

୭ଏଏ

The flat darkens as storm clouds press closer to land. As the wind increases, rain hits the window like pellets. The television screen flashes a black rain symbol and The Observatory advises all residents to remain indoors. A long gust of wind hits and the floor sways slightly under her feet. The building is modern. It will not fall.

David calls from Toronto. Their engagement began when she mentioned a year-long posting in the Hong Kong office. David asked without asking. It's logical, he explained, a way of going further in the relationship. She didn't know if she needed to respond, as it had already been decided. He produced an engagement ring that she doesn't wear; her fingers swell in the tropical heat.

On the phone they fill each other in on their separate plans for the weekend. David's heading out to dinner with friends, his Friday night; Sarah's a hostage to the weather, her Saturday morning.

"Black rain," explains Sarah.

"What's that?"

"Torrential rains, thunderstorms."

"You're having quite the adventure." David asks for more details of her daily life. He's more preoccupied with Hong Kong, the exotic, than with her. When will she disclose her acrophobia to David? He has a way of looking askance at personal weakness.

"Have you booked your ticket yet?" she asks.

"Bit of a problem. Something has come up. Big client meeting."

"But it's your turn to visit."

"It's my job, Sarah."

"I have a job too."

Silence on the phone.

Sarah pictures fibre-optic cables stretched beneath the Pacific Ocean. Miles and miles of cable roped across basins and mountainous ridges of the continental shelf, strung across deep oceanic trenches. Glass cables, the only solid connection between them. Transmitting silence.

David suggests they meet in Vancouver in mid-October, he's scheduled into a legal conference. She says she'll think about it. Near the end of the call, he asks if she's thought about a dress that would be suitable for the wedding.

"Not really."

"Have one tailor-made. We'll show it to the kids, tell them about the year Mommy lived in Hong Kong."

Mommy, thinks Sarah and hangs up. She's never thought of herself as a mother. It strikes her as entirely foreign.

Outside the kitchen window, clouds form graphite shapes so intense that they seem to instantaneously dissolve. Natural light recedes until there is nothing in the world but water. The refrigerator *click-clicks* in the darkness. She turns on all the lights.

She keeps herself busy into the afternoon, checks work email, cleans, rearranges her few belongings until she cannot cope with the sway any longer. The office, she thinks. Her work is located on the nineteenth floor and, for some reason, she can manage anything under twenty-five floors without resorting to duct tape.

Sarah drops to safety in the lift.

There are no taxis in the street and she starts walking. She's drenched in a moment. A wild gust of wind rips the skin off her umbrella. She dashes onto the Mid-Levels escalator and begins her descent into Central District. Partway down, rainwater leaks onto the moving platform and she exits early. Picks her way down tiled stairs to street level.

As she splashes across a narrow street, a taxi surges past and swamps her with a wave. She loses her balance and falls hard onto the curb, scrapes her knee. Stunned, she remains on the pavement, holds her breath until pain establishes itself into a regular-irregular rhythm.

A man emerges through a curtain of rain. He picks her up and hauls her onto her feet in one movement. She feels unsteady but hangs on. Blood mixed with water drips down her leg.

"Let me — "

"I don't need — "

"You're bleeding — "

The man steers her across a sandbagged doorway into an English-style pub and sets her, dripping, on a barstool. Dabbing her shredded knee with a drink napkin, he asks the bartender for a first-aid kit. "I'm Fast Eddy," he says and gently eases gauze over her bandage.

"Sarah."

"Swept away," says Fast Eddy.

"It was a big wave." Sarah hands him a piece of adhesive tape.

"A rogue wave," says Fast Eddy and grins up at her. An angular face, straight nose. Dishevelled dirty-blond hair above a thin blue T-shirt, the blue of twilight, more evening than night.

"You all right, then?" asks a pudgy Englishman propped up at the bar.

"Yes," says Sarah. She wonders if she will regain her balance in this precipitous city.

"Sarah doesn't need a man, Load Toad," says Fast Eddy.

"Women." Load Toad orders whiskey all around.

"Where'd you get a nickname like Load Toad?" asks Sarah.

"Don't ask," says Load Toad and grins.

Fast Eddy says, "You gotta admit that the initials are perfectly — "

"Perpendicular," says Sarah.

There are more waitstaff in the pub than patrons. The bartender wears a Bluetooth headset and is busy texting on his cellphone. One of the cooks is drinking a beer at the end of the bar. Heavy metal blares out of the jukebox.

"What are you doing out in a black rainstorm, Sarah?" asks Fast Eddy.

"Heading to work," says Sarah. "You?"

"Search and rescue," says Fast Eddy and shoots Load Toad a dirty look. "You?"

"Avoiding a perfect storm at home." Load Toad points out the window, a kinetic snapshot of driving rain. "Black rainstorms are worse than typhoons. Right bastards, they are."

"Flight I was on landed on the diagonal in the middle of a black rainstorm," says Fast Eddy.

"Life flash in front of your eyes?" asks Load Toad.

"Nope."

"Any regrets?" Sarah sips her whiskey. It tastes like smoke mixed with salt water.

"Oh, yeah," says Fast Eddy.

"Christ, who doesn't?" Load Toad gestures to the bartender for another round.

Fast Eddy shakes his head. A vein at his temple knots into a blue bruise. Sarah wonders what it would feel like beneath her tongue.

"You and your fucking two-drink rule," says Load Toad and orders two whiskeys. "Reckon I liked it better when you drank too much."

"Yeah," says Fast Eddy. "I didn't."

"It's pouring," says Sarah. She fingers the gauzy bandage on her knee and sets nerve endings on fire. Easing back in her barstool, she reminds herself to breathe through the pain. The burn of whiskey distracts.

Load Toad nudges Sarah with his shoulder and points across the street. "Neon over the butcher shop is lovely in the rain, isn't it? Pink light over BBQ ducks. Fucking brilliant."

"When will it end?" asks Sarah.

"Middle of September." Fast Eddy catches Sarah's eye and won't look away until she does. His eyes are dark green. The colour reminds her of seaweed.

"I have loved the air outside 7-Eleven on many a warm September night," says Load Toad and raises his glass. "Drinking beer from a can, smoking."

"Are you a poet?" asks Sarah.

"Nah. Potter." Load Toad relays a history of ceramics. Describes, in detail, the fusion of English pottery traditions with Japanese Raku. "Crockery's the fucking beauty. Functional. Made from clay, scorched with fire. Earth art, it is."

"What kind of work do you do?" Fast Eddy asks Sarah.

"I'm a consultant."

Load Toad snorts.

"Consultants work hard, Load Toad." Fast Eddy shoots another dirty look at him. He shifts in his seat and leans in her direction. She can feel him beside her, closer. She wonders if he is protecting her, then she wonders if she wants protecting.

"Try running a business in a fucking financial tsunami," says Load Toad. "Endless trips into Mainland China. Factory dust full of coal, Christ knows what else."

"Try a bank," says Fast Eddy. "After a fall from grace."

"It's true," says Load Toad and shifts his weight.

Sarah wonders about falling from grace. Wonders if she'd feel dizzy all the way down or just until the twenty-fifth floor. She gulps down a half glass of whiskey.

"Patience." Load Toad rubs fatigue out of his eyes.

"Been here eight years, still haven't any," says Fast Eddy.

"Try fifteen," says Load Toad. "Try marriage."

"I did." Fast Eddy rests his square jaw in his hand.

There's a beat of silence then Load Toad says, "Don't mind me, eh, Fast Eddy? Been drinking since Friday, lunch."

"What're your thoughts on The Suitable Dress?" asks Sarah. She has no idea why she asks except there's an uncomfortable tension growing between the two men. Besides she's drunk and facing another whiskey.

"Don't look good in a dress," says Load Toad.

Sarah nods. "I'm a pants girl."

"Always fancied a hat with flowers on the brim," says Load Toad.

Fast Eddy says, "I'd wear a dress."

"Is that a dare?" asks Load Toad. "Cause if it is — "

"You quit drinking, go home to the missus," says Fast Eddy. "I'll wear a dress."

"Deal." Load Toad smacks his hand down on the bar.

"Three weeks today," says Fast Eddy after checking his electronic schedule. "I'm out of town for a bit. Sourcing ladies clothing in my size takes time."

"Shop near the Cricket Club make ladies shoes, eh, Fast Eddy? Special order." Load Toad sketches directions onto a drink napkin.

"And you know this how?" asks Sarah.

"I know everything," says Load Toad and shrugs. "And nothing."

She takes a closer look at him. One of his sideburns is flattened against his cheek and the other flares out wildly. She tries to picture him in a hat and fails. "This I've got to see."

"Give me your digits." Load Toad stabs at his cellphone with a meaty forefinger. "I'll text you the particulars."

"What do you have in mind?" asks Fast Eddy.

"Bit of a party."

Fast Eddy shakes his head. "You're impossible."

"Old trick, new dogs, that." Load Toad grins like he can't help himself.

"My sandal's ripped." Sarah hops off her barstool, reaches down for her sandal, realizes that her knee should be throbbing but can't feel anything.

"What're you going to wear, Sarah?" asks Fast Eddy.

"I shall dress as a suitable man," says Sarah and steadies herself.

"Christ, what's that?" Load Toad asks Fast Eddy.

"I figure that out, I'll let you know." Fast Eddy runs his hand over the scarred wood bar top like he's feeling his way across a familiar surface. Sarah pictures his hand running up her calf into the private space behind her knee.

"What's it like, being a girl?" asks Load Toad.

"There are expectations." Sarah's cheeks feel flushed.

"Try being a boy." Load Toad drains his drink. He stands, pushes his stool away from the bar and asks, "Think the missus will open the door?"

"Maybe."

"I'm in trouble."

"Go home, big man." Fast Eddy telephones his car service.

A few minutes later, he pours Load Toad into a black Mercedes, provides instructions to his driver, and waits until the car pulls away. He turns, pushes his fingers through his wet hair, and darker roots emerge.

The wash of the rain down the window distorts Sarah's view out on to the street. Fast Eddy's shirt, the blue of night, is plastered to his lean torso.

"Sure you don't need a man?" asks Fast Eddy when he returns to the bar.

"Yes," says Sarah and means no. She swirls whiskey around her glass like a man and takes Fast Eddy back to her flat.

෴ ෴ ෴

Sarah watches Fast Eddy sleep. Fatigue pools under his eyes like smog. She wonders how he can sleep in a swaying building. They're thirty-four floors above solid ground. At any moment they could be sucked across parquet flooring, thrown against single pane glass and fall to their deaths.

Sarah tries not to think about the eighteen maids and four children who've perished this year, tumbling out of open windows. The maids leaning out, wiping the window exteriors into a shine, overreaching. The children, playing in window seats, dropping a toy and chasing after it. Sarah tries not to think of children and toys, falling in tandem.

Instead she thinks about her upcoming wedding and The Suitable Dress. She thinks about the woman scheduled to wear it. She wakes Fast Eddy and says, "We can't see each other again."

"Mmmhmm," says Fast Eddy. He props himself up onto his elbow.

"I'm vertiginous — "

"Tell me what you want, Sarah." Fast Eddy reaches for her, caresses the vulnerable aspect of her waist, between rib and hip. The ambiguous space between men and women.

Sarah has no idea how to answer because no one has ever asked her what she wants.

"This?" asks Fast Eddy. "Or this?"

"This," says Sarah and shows him.

Rain slides down the window like a screen.

ॐ ॐ ॐ

After several nights with Fast Eddy in her bed, Sarah makes an appointment with a well-regarded dressmaker. She arrives at the tiny shop early and edges past a row of antique mannequins who wait patiently for their next customers. Newspaper headlines circling, the mannequins' small waists are defined by old news.

The shop is empty but Sarah hears voices in the back.

She surveys the sample rack. A Mao suit made of silk seems incongruous. She tries on an old-fashioned cheongsam in what she thinks is her size. Too tight across the shoulders, it flattens her breasts.

The dressmaker emerges from the back and joins Sarah at the mirror.

"Un-good," says the dressmaker and scrunches up her nose.

The dressmaker pulls bolt after bolt of Chinese silk from glass cases: white, off-white, ivory. She points out slight variations in weight, texture, and sheen. Sarah traces semicircles stamped into fabric and tries to focus on their differences. David recommends suitable clothing; Fast Eddy removes it at every opportunity. Double un-good.

Sarah selects a crepe satin. Shaking her head, the dressmaker selects another then drapes a length of ivory duchesse satin across her body. The two women scrutinize Sarah's image in the tri-fold mirror. Washed out. Sarah resolves never to see Fast Eddy again.

As the dressmaker takes her measurements, she reaches from behind and lightly cups Sarah's breasts with both hands and says, "Too big." Her lips twitch with displeasure and Sarah wonders if the dressmaker expects a smaller version to emerge on command.

Sarah thinks about the images of near-naked women plastered across any available space in Hong Kong. About the swarms of scantily clad women that walk the streets. About the heat and how she cannot bear clothing against her skin. With each passing day, she sheds more layers and enjoys the freedom. On the street, men and women alike stare at her breasts.

The dressmaker's hands linger. Sarah's nipples harden. For a moment she wonders what disapproval would taste like. This moment, and her thoughts, will not be shared in her next telephone call with David. On impulse, Sarah orders a trouser suit made of green shantung silk, textured.

"You order wedding dress?"

"Next time," says Sarah. She leaves the cluttered shop.

"Hurry, hurry," the dressmaker calls after her on the street.

On the crowded walkway leading to the Star Ferry, a beggar sleeps sitting up. He wears a ragged blue tunic. Sarah places several coins in a battered coffee tin on the pavement. The beggar startles, raises his head from his knees. Blue eyes emerge below matted hair.

"I've lost my money," he says. "Every bloody cent."

"You should call your family."

"Where've they gone?"

Sarah doesn't know what to tell him.

A green light flashes ahead. The Star Ferry bangs against the pier and water sprays. The boatman whistles and signals final boarding. Sarah dashes down the passage and makes the ramp just in time.

๛ ๛ ๛

The Globe. 8'ish, reads Load Toad's text. Fast Eddy leaves a message that he'll stop by her flat and pick her up on his way. Sarah doesn't call him back.

Sarah tells herself she isn't going to the pub and dresses anyway. She wears her new green trouser suit and a pair of ridiculously high heels. Before she knows it, Fast Eddy is at her door. He's wearing a blue wrap dress that gapes at the neck, and jewelled flip-flops.

In the living room, Sarah strikes what she believes to be a masculine pose. He shakes his head and says, "You make a good-looking man. Love the shoes."

"Suitable?"

"Like I said. I'll let you know," says Fast Eddy. As he tells her about his business trip to the United States, he looks even more tired than when she last saw him.

Sarah longs to lick the silk that lines his mouth, put her hands on his body. Instead she tells him about the beggar on the walkway to the Star Ferry. "He had an English accent."

"A banker. Jeremy something or other. Lost everything at the track, including funds from the bank," says Fast Eddy. "What were you doing, Kowloon-side?"

"Visiting a dressmaker," says Sarah. "Had this suit made up. The dressmaker did the strangest thing — "

"Who's David?"

"How — "

"You talk in your sleep."

She doesn't want to tell him but tells him anyway.

"What do you want, Sarah?"

His words drop down through her.

"It's your call," says Fast Eddy.

Sarah thinks about submerged fibre-optic cables, the silence that stretches. Do glass cables make a sound when they break underwater?

"I've made a lot of mistakes." Fast Eddy tightens the strap of his wrap dress in an attempt to fix the gaping neckline. His clavicle hangs out, a ridge of bone that crests into his broad shoulder. He seems more exposed than he is. Vulnerable.

"Were you dizzy?" asks Sarah. "When you fell from grace?"

"Nope. I'm dizzy now. Every single day, Sarah. Wouldn't have it any other way."

Sarah crosses the vertigo line.

RICHARD

YELLOW HARD HATS swarm over the Star Ferry Terminal demolition site, forty-two floors below. You don't mind the destruction of the terminal. The plain concrete box, with green marine paint that bubbles and lifts in the humidity, is unattractive. Reminds you of a bunker.

A cart clatters in the hallway.

"*Yum cha?*" asks the Tea Lady.

Don't turn away from the corner office window. Fine days are few, between a high pollution index and extreme weather. Intense heat, black rainstorms, typhoons, and landslides. Precisely why you moved to Hong Kong. Predictably unpredictable.

The Tea Lady mutters under her breath.

"I beg your pardon?" Take in a nondescript, middle-aged woman wearing a too-large Marks and Spencer jumper. Titanium eyeglasses frame her dark eyes. She doesn't answer. When she pushes a full glass of tea in your direction, her jade bracelets rattle together. Take the steaming tumbler and quickly deposit it on your desk, but not before it scalds your fingers.

The Tea Lady shoves her cart along to the next office.

As the tea cools, skim the paper and pause on an article about a Star Ferry protestor on a hunger strike. You can appreciate a stand on the necessity of restoration works but why would anyone starve himself over a peeling, green bunker? Still tender from the hot glass of tea, your fingertips tingle when you press them against the ridges of your pants.

It's dark when you leave the office.

The bars and restaurants in the entertainment district are overflowing. It's the first week of December. The music that blares out sounds louder, more cheerful than usual. As if the owners know their patrons need something more at Christmas, something that reminds them of home. Home. Have your tenants prepared the garden for winter? You've emailed to remind them but haven't heard back.

Stop for a drink. Select the bar with a bright-green fronting and hanging baskets of red poinsettias. Pushing through the crowd, watch the bartender pull down an assortment of bottles before settling into a rhythm of measuring and pouring, filling a sizeable drink order. When he's available, order a vodka martini. Bit of a Christmas splurge.

Settle on a stool at the end of the long bar next to a burly man wearing a blue velvet vest. The man ignores you. Checking your Blackberry for messages, you find your in-box empty. It would be prudent to walk back to the flat and prepare for your regularly scheduled 1:00 AM conference call. That's when the New York Stock Exchange opens, Hong Kong time. You're lucky not to answer to anyone these days, particularly with these middle-of-the-night conference calls.

One drink and straight home.

Richard

Two women in red-silk cheongsams walk in and join two men in dark business suits. They pair off in a booth in the back. Red, black, red, black. Predictably unpredictable profits. Lately you're worried about trends emerging in the stock markets, experiencing a persistent sense of impending doom.

Your vodka martini arrives with a cranberry and orange garnish. As you sip, examine the crowd through the bar mirrors lining the walls of the long narrow room. A pudgy Englishman at the front of the bar breaks into song and waves his cigarette in the air, punctuating the chorus with a smouldering ember. His mates laugh and join in. Sounds like "The Fairytale of New York". You regularly travel to New York on business and don't care for it. London is a proper city, particularly at Christmas.

Picture London's cityscape and how beautiful the Parliament is at Christmastime. Pure white lights profile the stately buildings, reflecting them onto the Thames. You prefer their order and symmetry to the gaudy light shows on Oxford and Regent where Disney characters float above the streets. This is your first Christmas away from London and you booked a Christmas lunch at The Ritz-Carlton to compensate. If only you could find a stall with roasted chestnuts.

A beautiful young woman wearing tight jeans inches past on high heels. She tilts into your shoulder and apologizes without smiling. Young people these days have no manners. Blue Vest closely watches her progress in the bar mirror. When a tray of glasses drops somewhere in the background, the bartender frowns into whatever drink he's pouring.

Ask the bartender how he remembers all the drink recipes.

"They're listed on my cellphone," the bartender says without looking up.

A noisy group of expatriate women are tucked in the corner booth. A table of six, martini glasses raised in celebration, speaking all at once. Englishwomen, professional types by the looks of it. Drain your martini. Try not to think about the professional Englishwoman to whom you used to be married.

The music blares louder.

Signal the bartender. "I'll have a — "

"Gin tonic," says the bartender. "Coming up."

"How did you know?"

"An educated guess," he says and pours two fingers of gin into a tall glass.

Blue Vest sits there staring into his pint. Clearly he isn't a conversationalist. No worries, there's always the crowd. The bar is packed. The patrons inch through the long, narrow room. Moving in a slow circuit, in front of the bar and down to the booths in the rear and back again, they ease past, sizing one another up before spilling out onto the street.

A flower seller slips through the doorway, his arms filled with a tangle of exotic blooms. You rarely bought flowers for your wife and wonder if that was part of the problem. One day last January, she called you an old man. You're so predictable, she said at breakfast over the financial section. You never do anything out of the ordinary. Strange for, at the time, you'd seriously considered taking up photography as a hobby. You didn't ask her what she meant. She left shortly thereafter.

Order another gin tonic.

A jade plant squats on the floor beside the bar. Sturdy branches with clumps of leaves curved like waxy fingertips. You wonder what substance would squirt out if its leaves were squished, or if they're empty.

Richard

An attractive Englishwoman from the noisy corner booth squeezes up to the bar. She flags the bartender immediately, calls out her order, her deeply tanned hand drumming while she waits. She appears substantial. You could do with someone substantial. You aren't going to ask her to join you.

You ask her to join you.

She refuses.

Professional Englishwomen.

Has your wife received your change of address notification card from Hong Kong? You haven't heard from her since she filed for divorce. Never do anything out of the ordinary.

When you check your Blackberry for messages again, a petite woman carrying a designer shopping bag staggers past. "Excuse me," she says and smiles. Her crimson-tipped hand lightly rests on your arm.

"No worries, no worries."

"I like this bar," she says. "Do you?"

Clear your throat. Her accent is quite charming.

The petite woman's hand lingers. She remains standing close.

"Used to be mine," says Blue Vest. His voice is loud.

"I beg your pardon?"

"The bar," says Blue Vest. "It used to be mine."

"What happened?"

"A bar girl is what happened." Blue Vest shoots the petite woman a dirty look like she's the one responsible.

"Excuse me," she says. As she turns away, her face is pale, drawn. She finds a space down the bar and hangs her shopping bag on a hook under the ledge. Her small handbag rests in the bottom of the otherwise empty shopping bag.

After Blue Vest drains his glass, he launches into a rambling story involving a bar girl, secret boyfriends and a large sum of money. Recounting his story seems to exhaust him and he slumps into his stool even more. The bartender automatically slides a full pint in his direction.

You don't know how to respond.

You've heard about expatriate men involving themselves with bar girls. Stories abound. When you first arrived, a couple coworkers dragged you to a girlie bar and offered to engage the services of a girl on your behalf. You're divorced, aren't you? Go have fun, they said. You decided against it. Too many health risks.

The music blares louder still.

The crowd has stopped moving. It's as if everyone has found his or her place for the evening. The singing Englishman with the cigarette stands up on the rungs of his barstool, leans forward, shouts for the bartender, and in doing so, knocks his drink over. Laughing, his mates haul him back into a seated position and apologize. The bartender smiles and nods as he wipes up the mess.

The beautiful young woman, the one in tight jeans and high heels, flirts with an older man sporting a clean-shaven head. They're propped up against one another in an intimate fashion. He's seated and the beautiful woman stands between his legs, leans into his shoulder. When he caresses her waist and then lower still, she laughs an open-throated kind of laugh and kisses him.

Avert your eyes.

Blue Vest appears to be sleeping, suspended above his half-full pint, velvet stretched across his paunch. Farther down the bar, the petite woman is nursing what's left of a cola. She fidgets with her collar, smoothes it over her carefully ironed blouse, red fingertips floating over white cotton.

Think about her neat appearance. Think about her accent, about how different her voice sounds. Maybe you don't want anyone who talks like the Englishwoman to whom you used to be married. The year prior your wife begged for a holiday to Majorca over Christmas. Just the two of us, she said. Lying by the pool, enjoying a glass of white wine. But Christmas is a time for tradition, you said. The matter was settled. You stayed home.

The jade plant leans to one side, its shallow roots exposed. Cigarette butts are crushed into the parched soil. People don't pay adequate care and attention to the greenery. Resolve to send another email to your tenants, remind them to attend to your front garden.

A couple of the Englishwomen from the corner booth try to flag the bartender and fail to catch his attention. As they wait, you shift in their direction. Are they talking about you?

"Linen in London, corduroy in the tropics."

"Oh, he's harmless, isn't he? Leave him alone."

સ-સ-સ

Are you going to stop at the convenience store and buy something sweet? You're partial to glazed coconut tarts. If you're lucky, you find a little sliver of maraschino cherry and you enjoy the bright-red, sugary crescent, even if it sticks in your teeth.

No. This evening you walk past the harshly lit store and climb the stairs to your colonial-style flat, empty-handed. The flat is stuffy. You could open the windows but don't; there are mosquitoes and other insects. Instead you press the button for the air-conditioning and switch on the hall lights.

Professional Englishwomen. Check your appearance in the hall mirror. Not bad. You're tanned from outdoor tennis but appear older than forty-six, probably from your never-ending schedule of late-night conference calls with New York.

Mix a largish gin tonic.

Your Blackberry rings at 1:00 AM sharp. As you talk banking with your US counterparts, you squish your blistered fingertips and nothing emerges. Peel the dead skin away until blood wells, drips down your fingers onto your trousers.

Rephrasing Kate

OFF TO ONE side, kneeling on the cool steps of the open-air hotel lobby in Bali, a woman twists bamboo leaves into little rectangular baskets. Her head bends over her working hands, her posture erect; the creamy soles of her feet curve up behind her in an inverted *S*. Kate watches from a distance and, curiosity piqued, approaches. "What are you making?"

"Baskets, Missus. For offerings." The weaver smiles slightly. Her face seems vaguely threatening yet her eyes are gentle and filled with a diffuse light. "Tomorrow, we thank the gods for machines."

"Machines?"

"Machines. Cars, telephones, computers. All machines." She carefully folds several long leaves and snips the excess away with a pair of hand-forged shears. Sharp-edged bamboo confetti flickers to the ground.

"May I?" asks Kate.

The weaver presents a completed basket for inspection.

Kate examines the intricate woven structure. The corners are faultless and the finishing cuts even, given its small size. It's a remarkable sample. "How long does it take?"

"How long?" The weaver appears confused, places a half-finished basket under her arm and holds her hands a few inches apart in an approximation.

I am forever rephrasing, thinks Kate. Making myself understood. "How many minutes?"

"Not long, Missus."

Kate wonders if she will wake to offerings on her bedside table in the morning. She is, after all, a computer waiting for physical information to analyze. To compensate she fills her days with activities. Runs assorted errands connected with her current decoration project. Dinner with Alan if he is in the city, alone if he is travelling.

She is on her own a great deal and has taken to talking to herself in the too-quiet flat. "Another glass of wine, Kate?" She nods in agreement before pouring a second glass and, more often than not, a third. Patterns of three.

"Do you like making these baskets?"

"Of course. I am blessed. Many people has no jobs after the bombings," says the weaver politely, even formally. Her eyes darken. The whole time her hands are braiding and folding bamboo.

The two women size up one another. Then a volley of animal screeching erupts in the distance and breaks the tension. "Sacred monkeys, very naughty. They steal." The weaver disapprovingly shakes her head and waves in the direction of a deep ravine.

Gazing down at the heavy canopy of trees, Kate thinks it unlikely that the monkeys would steal from her because she is invisible. She has no career, unless trailing behind her husband constitutes as one. Two international moves in three years. She speculates about emerging technologies. Who would hire her after three years out of the oil and gas industry?

"You like dance?" the weaver asks, suddenly returning to her earlier friendlier tone. "I make arrangement. Dinner dance at restaurant. Tomorrow-night-dinner. Very nice to you." Without waiting for Kate's response, the weaver rises and disappears into the back office.

Kate is alone in the lobby. The small hotel consists of a gathering of traditional, thatched guesthouses situated high on a hill above the Monkey Forest. The grounds climb up and down; stone pathways and staircases disappear between the wooden houses.

Car wheels grind gravel. Wondering if her driver has finally arrived, Kate strides over and peers down a steep flight of stairs to the driveway below. She spots several suitcases and overhears male voices speaking in Indonesian. Then a uniformed driver pushes the wrought-iron gate open and a man enters.

He is tall and his head is shaved. Carrying a large computer case across his chest, his step is precise, light, and he climbs easily. Halfway up the stairs, he glances up at Kate and grins. Kate fights the urge to grin back.

He arrives on the landing.

"Decker," he says. An American voice.

"Pardon me?"

"I'm Decker." A striped shirt glares beneath a business jacket. Kate introduces herself.

The weaver emerges from the back office and warmly greets Decker. Again, her face is vaguely menacing and that's when Kate notices that something is missing from her smile. The points of her eyeteeth are ground flat. The weaver bows deeply then captures Decker's hand between her palms.

Decker speaks to her in Indonesian.

The weaver responds in English. "Yes, Mister Decker, is ready. You lose weight? I order black rice pudding for you, tomorrow-morning-breakfast."

"Yeah, right. I'm eating too well." Laughing, Decker runs his hands over his firm stomach. Long, slender fingers and manicured fingernails. Kate thinks his touch would be surprisingly light for a man his size. Catching her eye he says, "She makes me speak English every single time. What can I do?"

The weaver moues. "I practice English."

"Your English is good. It's my Indonesian that sucks," says Decker.

"Your Indonesian very good to you."

"How's the design course going?" Decker asks the weaver.

"I build website. Mr. Decker, please. You look?"

"Yeah, sure, show me tomorrow."

The weaver appears pleased as she works on various registration forms.

"Where you from?" asks Decker in Kate's direction.

"Hong Kong. You?"

"Same, same." Decker removes his jacket and rolls up his shirt sleeves. A fishtail curves across one forearm, its iridescent orange scales shimmering with sweat. A crab scuttles across his other forearm and dives for cover beneath striped cotton.

"Who you here with?" asks Kate automatically.

"The big company that shall not be named," says Decker. Impatiently he pats his suit jacket pockets, searching for and finding a rumpled package of Marlboro's and a large metallic Zippo lighter.

Ignored, thinks Kate and turns away so she doesn't say something rude. Some days she can't believe she's the same person who mapped deposits and fault trends deep beneath the surface. Who recommended major projects. These days she's off-shored to the table with the wives. Kate grips her handbag tight until the handles pinch her fingers and reminds herself that she is a white woman in Asia. Sexually redundant.

Her driver finally arrives.

Decker turns to Kate. "A car? It's a fifteen minute walk into Ubud," he says, a hard edge in his voice roughened further by a steady stream of cigarette smoke. "Just cut through the Monkey Forest."

૭ૐ ૭ૐ ૭ૐ

"Stop the car," says Kate when she spots the large signpost that announces the Monkey Forest. After instructing her driver to deliver her packages to the hotel, she enters the gateway and walks into a wooded twilight. The jungle closes over her and Kate watches the long slow sway of treetops high above her. No wind permeates the canopy.

Signs identifying various species of birds and trees are nailed to the occasional tree. Kate ignores them and moves downhill where a few tourists congregate around a hulking banyan tree. Hurrying, she avoids banana peels, rotten lettuces, and other unrecognizable food debris smeared into the pavement. A few monkeys squat along the stone walls. Arriving at the banyan, Kate stops and watches several small silver-haired ones perched above.

A larger monkey with an oozing gash on his flattened nose swivels his head in Kate's direction and stares, unblinking, at her for a long time. His eyes are full of some emotion Kate cannot make out. The monkey bares his teeth and hisses loudly, spit flying. Immediately the other males jump, rebounding off branches, and then drop to the ground. On the pathway they scatter, circling one another, and a series of attacks and retaliations erupt. Off to one side, a baby monkey cries until one of the larger ones snatches his hand and drags him into the safety of the underbrush.

Kate freezes, then escapes up the pathway. From a safe distance, she turns back. The wounded monkey is sitting at the deserted base of the banyan tree. He stares intently after her. Kate walks back to the hotel as fast as possible in the stifling heat.

༔ ༔ ༔

Kate tosses in her empty bed and, sometime after midnight, drifts into a shallow sleep. Decker enters her dreams, lying below her in the wide hotel bed, thrusting up to meet her, and he tells her something important and, for some reason, she cannot understand him.

Pleasure clusters deep within and she begins to orgasm. Decker laughs and little purple-and-orange crabs crawl out of his gaping mouth, scrabble across the white sheets, onto the tiled floor, underneath the bed. Then the sound of a huge door slamming from somewhere deep in the earth smashes against the night.

Awake and sweating, Kate lies in her bed, her heart galloping. The guesthouse sways, wooden beams creaking. She jumps out of bed and, standing on trembling floorboards, locks her knees in an effort to keep her balance. At the window, large branches are whipping back and forth, leaves snapping inside out.

Long moments pass before the ground settles into a static hum. An atmospheric heaviness presses down on her. The ravine rings, a cacophony of animal noises; the only sounds Kate clearly differentiates are peacocks screaming. Panicking, she rushes out the door, through the garden and up steep stairs, across the spiky grass toward the now candlelit lobby.

There on the lowest step of the lobby stands a uniformed security guard and Decker, quietly talking together in Indonesian. Their words rustle in the darkness. Decker turns toward her. "No worries," he says, his voice steady. "A small tremor."

"What magnitude?"

"A small tremor. Nothing to worry about."

The security guard says something and sweeps an arc of light over her. She is acutely aware she is standing there in a flimsy nightgown and her gaze slips, settling on a vague spot on Decker's broad shoulder. A flush heats her cheeks.

Decker hands her an industrial-strength black flashlight. "Just in case you need it, Kate."

"You remember my name." She finds herself blinking back tears that she isn't expecting, embarrassed more by revealing her emotions than her body.

"Yeah, sure," says Decker.

Kate flees back to her guesthouse, tells herself that it was a small tremor, a magnitude no greater than blowing a seismic charge. The peacocks scream in the dark.

ॐॐॐ

Kate sets out on foot for the dance performance. As she hurries up onto the main road, her heels catch in the gravel. She walks past several compounds surrounded by high stone walls. Moonlight shines off the glass shards embedded along the tops. A radio plays. Kate speculates what else lies beyond the walls. When the moon goes missing she wishes she'd brought along Decker's flashlight.

The sprawling restaurant is comprised of raised pavilions scattered around a central courtyard, each building contains two or three tables and Kate's is no exception. A table of six, glasses raised in some kind of celebration, next to hers. Speaking some Northern European language. They nod in her direction.

Near the end of dinner, a large stack of firewood in the courtyard is doused with an accelerant and lit. The wind surges and Kate smells the stench of gasoline. The emerging stars hang low in the soft dark sky, casting their own shadows as if double exposed. How unfamiliar the stars appear; their light is diffuse and yellow, unlike the hard white stars back home.

A flickering torch appears in the rice fields, then another and yet another. The men materialize behind the torchbearers, their heads bobbing. Single file, in two columns, one hundred men traverse the narrow footpaths between watery fields. Hoarse and raucous, the frogs announce the men passing.

The long lines converge and the men, young and old, approach the whirling bonfire. Bare-chested, they wear black-and-white checked sarongs and a black head wrap with a single, red hibiscus tucked in the folds. The men sit cross-legged, pressed close to one another, forming tight concentric circles around a small stage. Flames leap and skin glistens in the firelight. The men wait with eyes downcast. Even the sky holds its breath.

The narrator calls and the story begins. The men sway in unison, chanting: *kechak, kechak*. A heavily jewelled Princess with a sideways stare edges by and gazes over her shoulder at the Demon King, who is stalking her from the rice *padi* beyond. The glittering Princess is caught and imprisoned on a golden throne and off in the distance, her Prince roars in outrage. The chorus responds by leaning in, beating their chests and calling, louder and louder: *kechak, keCHAK*.

The Monkey God materializes out of nowhere, his body smeared with ashes. He embarks on a rigorous journey to rescue the Princess. Kate cannot take her eyes off the Monkey God as he celebrates. He leaps and staggers through the men. Dozens of ornate, silver bracelets band his upper arms, forcing his arms up into the air. With heavy eyebrows and contorted mouth, he brandishes a sword and flashes messages to the night sky. The chorus leans in, reaching for him and the Monkey God bounds away, tail jerking. The chanting fractures into a frenzied counterpoint: *KeCHAK, KECHAK, KECHAK*.

Then the chorus disintegrates. Several men fall to the ground, exhausted. Others wander the stage in a trance, back and forth, back and forth. No patterns emerge in their erratic movements. Kate calms herself by staring into the roaring bonfire.

❦❦❦

Later that evening, overlooking the ravine, Kate wonders where Alan is, what he is doing in a city full of beautiful women whom he never mentions. Then again there are a number of things she never mentions. Granitic extrusions, she thinks and realizes that, even though she's living on the hardest bedrock in the world, she isn't on solid ground.

Kate turns back to garden pathways curving around a swimming pool that glows like a stratigraphic time-slice. A lighter flares and a cigarette dances in the darkness. The wind whispers: *kechak*.

A striped shirt floats toward her.

"Why are you here, Kate?"

"To get away. You?"

"Trying to be good. What do you do?" Decker exhales a lazy O.

"To be good?"

Decker laughs. "No, your job."

"I used to be a geophysicist. You?"

"Communications." He pulls a beer out of an ice bucket stashed beneath a poolside table and pushes a slippery can into her empty hands. "Tell me about your job, Kate."

"I analyze seismic maps and search for patterns underground; find oil and gas deposits," says Kate and takes a seat at the table.

"How cool is that." Decker settles into a chair across from her, leans back and stares into the soft darkness above. "Look at the stars. I can't remember the last time I saw so many. You never see any in Hong Kong."

"I can't read the constellations," says Kate, smoothing her skirt over her knees. "Underground formations are my specialty."

"There are star charts. You like maps, don't you? You'd better get on it, Kate," says Decker.

Kate laughs.

"Jesus, it's hot." Decker removes his shirt, exposing a smooth hairless chest, and his tattoos emerge. On one arm, a reddish-gold carp climbs a waterfall up his flowering shoulder and on the other, crabs climb up into cherry blossoms. A green-scaled coil curves around one side of his waist. There's a creature that lives on his back.

"Your tattoos are remarkable."

"What do you see?" Decker carefully folds and drapes his shirt over the arm of his chair.

"Transformation," says Kate. "Do you map out your tattoos?"

"I figure it out as I go."

"Does it hurt?"

"You get used to it."

"The colours remind me of waveform classification."

"What's that?"

"Images of formations. Anomalies, specifically."

"That's me. Anomalous." His stare is impenetrable, both hard and soft. "You must be good at your job, Kate."

"I used to be."

A lizard skitters across flagstones.

"What are you doing here?" says Decker.

"I told you — "

"Getting away from the bright lights of Hong Kong." He considers the burning tip of his cigarette and grimaces. "Same, same. I've developed some bad habits."

"What kind?"

"Bar girls. There are none in Ubud, thank Christ," says Decker, as if he wishes it wasn't the case. He pauses. "Listen Kate, you gotta be careful in Asia. You don't want to spend all your time hanging around with a buncha *tai-tais*, getting into all kinds of trouble when their husbands are out of town."

"So you've heard."

"Yeah, you could say that." Decker laughs and tosses back his beer.

Quiet stretches between them.

Then Decker asks, "How many men you screwed since you got married, Kate?" The lizard freezes on the railing, fixed in silver light, eyes glittering like amphiboles. "C'mon, you can tell me. I just admitted I'm addicted to bar girls, for chrissakes." Decker taps cigarette ashes into the garden. The tendons along his wrist and hand are taut, well defined in the moonlight.

Kate thinks she has arrived here for some reason. Here at the pavilion on the grounds of this small hotel, here on the faulted ground above a deep ravine. Natural fractures enhance permeability. "Patterns of three," says Kate.

"What?"

"Three. I've slept with three men."

"Affairs?"

"One night stands." If you could call them that, they never stayed the night exactly. She didn't have to ask them to leave. They simply dressed and walked out of anonymous hotel rooms, pulling the doors shut behind them. Above a thick layer of rhyolite.

"You know, it's funny," says Decker quietly. "All that time I spent with bar girls, what I craved most was a regular conversation. A couple of months ago, I figure I'm ready to go on a regular date, with a regular woman, and the weirdest fucking thing happened. I discover I can't talk anymore. I mean. I can't connect."

"I'm sorry," says Kate.

"Yeah, give me a month or two and I'll get over myself. Meantime, night's a puppy." Decker removes the remainder of his clothing. He turns his back and a scorch-eyed, winged green dragon emerges, tail writhing in a sea of half-finished waves.

Rephrasing Kate

Mesmerized by incomplete waveforms, Kate searches for stable patterns and finds none. Geological confusion. Decker dives into the glowing pool in a single, fluid movement and, as he swims, the outline of his body shimmers one way and then the other.

21:23

THE NIGHT PORTER arrives earlier than usual and knocks twice.

Load Toad swings the door open.

Two women, hand in hand, stare down at their feet.

"Too much, parenthetically speaking," says Load Toad and shakes his head.

The Night Porter narrows his eyes and says, "Long Live the Chinese People." An old-fashioned military button on the breast pocket of his new uniform sags, and a blue thread dangles.

An hour later, the Night Porter returns with a young man.

"Christ," says Load Toad and grins. "I don't swing that way."

The Night Porter smiles.

Trapped at The Skyline Business Hotel on account of a stalled contract, and no cigarettes. Load Toad's sworn off smoking and tries to forget the large bottle of duty-free rum tucked in his luggage. Next door, The American turns up the television.

The next evening, a single knock, forceful.

The Night Porter gestures at the young woman next to him and says, "Yes, yes?"

The woman has no face.

Load Toad slams the door.

৵৵৵

On the way to the client's office, Load Toad's taxi skirts the partially constructed Guangzhou TV Tower. It is a slender hourglass of twisted steel columns that cinches at the waist like a corset. At the base lie mounds of concrete rubble from demolished apartment buildings, assorted construction debris, and abandoned trash.

Offerings to the future, thinks Load Toad.

The taxi slows in heavy traffic.

Red-and-white striped, plastic sheeting circles the construction site. An immense yellow machine shoves the debris, bullies it into oversized dump trucks that line the narrow streets. The taxi comes to a halt and the driver turns up the already blaring radio. From this angle, Load Toad isn't certain if the TV Tower relays or blocks information, but he has a hunch she's hiding something up her skirts.

A three-legged dog emerges through tattered sheeting and barks a warning at the stalled traffic. A man edges past on a motorcycle, a battered plastic container of water strapped to his seat with fluorescent bungee cords. As the motorcyclist navigates potholes, it shifts and water sloshes into the dusty street.

Load Toad checks his Blackberry for messages. Nothing pressing, just a short email from his wife reminding him of an increase in school fees. More money. Load Toad drums his fingers on his knee. More.

৵৵৵

Another futile day of contract negotiations ends in a stalemate. On his way through the hotel lobby, Load Toad notices The American alone at the bar and joins him.

"What d'you think of The Skyline Business Hotel?" asks Load Toad then places his drink order.

"There are tomatoes in my fruit basket," says The American.

"Tomatoes?"

"Cherry tomatoes. And they're completely covered in wax."

"Christ," says Load Toad.

The American shakes his balding head. He's wearing a faded T-shirt that announces Princeton University.

"Move 'em around," says Load Toad.

"Behind the door? That sort of thing?"

"Nah. March 'em across the floor. Military style."

The men laugh together.

The bartender turns up the volume on the television, a variety show with a bunch of clowns hopping across a watery obstacle course. The clowns all fall in, one after another, while the host laughs maniacally.

"They're filming the story of my life," says Load Toad. "Two weeks in China trying to close this deal. Two fucking weeks."

The American says, "Tell me about it."

After a while Load Toad asks, "Ever wonder what it'd be like, moving home?"

"The States? Economy's in the toilet."

"Yeah. Same in Britain. Bloody recession."

"You got it," says The American.

"We're sky-lined at The Skyline Hotel," says Load Toad. He smoothes down his rumpled dress shirt and reminds himself to send his dirty clothes to the hotel laundry.

The American lights a cigarette.

"My old man died last month," says Load Toad and bums a smoke. "Massive heart attack. Couldn't get out of China in time for his funeral."

The American waves at the bartender for another round.

"My sister sent me a letter, describing the service. Hilarious."

"Hilarious?" says The American.

"Yeah. Bunch of midgets showed up."

"Midgets."

"Masons," says Load Toad. "The old man was a member. Grand Master. Big man in charge."

"Of midgets or masons?"

"Both," says Load Toad and describes a long line of vertically challenged elderly men who, one by one, limped up to rest a hand on the old man's coffin. Murmured some kind of an ancient prayer, a benediction, no one knew.

"Midgets," says The American like he can't quite believe it.

"With disabilities," says Load Toad.

The men laugh until they cry.

"To your old man," says The American.

"A right bastard," says Load Toad and they clink glasses.

"What's your best memory?"

"Drinking beer in the shed, talking footie," says Load Toad. He pictures his old man crammed into a rusty camp chair, coils of green hosepipe at his feet.

The American nods. "My old man cemented *everything*. Covered the front yard in the '80s."

"There was a recession in the '80s, eh?"

"You got it."

"Fortifications," says Load Toad. "Makes sense to me."

The American doesn't say anything in response.

Load Toad asks, "Your old man still alive?"

"Ten years," says The American and points up.

"Sidelined at The Hotel in the Sky," says Load Toad.

રુ*રુ*રુ*

In his room, Load Toad removes the bottle of Bacardi from his luggage and carefully places it on top of the lacquered television cabinet.

There's a sound outside.

When he opens the door, The Woman with No Face is standing there, alone. No Night Porter. In a moment of weakness, Load Toad lets her in. Sitting at the end of his bed, she touches him, talks to him in Cantonese about his future.

A fire alarm rings in the hallway.

"Yeah. Don't worry," says Load Toad. "It rings for me."

The Woman with No Face carefully folds her small hands, lotus buds, in her lap. Her movements are so beautiful, Load Toad's throat aches.

They evacuate the hotel. In the stairwell, his next-door neighbour, The American, the one who leaves his television on all night, says, "She's very pretty." Load Toad nods and, when they reach the street, sends The Woman with No Face away.

The fire brigade arrives and Load Toad catches a glimpse of The Night Porter in a speaking role he has never seen him in. The Night Porter barks orders at firemen and hotel staff alike. His voice is loud, abrasive. When curious bystanders in the street file past to catch a glimpse, he barks at them too.

No fire exists.

When the fire brigade departs, the siren is silent but the flashing lights are on. The Night Porter gives the all-clear and hotel patrons return to the building. As Load Toad winds through the crowded lobby, he thinks he should never have let The Woman with No Face in.

The tape on the sleeve of the Bacardi sticks but Load Toad persists. Glass of amber liquid in hand, he tries not to worry about his contract and reminds himself to review Perfect Order Measurement in the morning.

☙ ☙ ☙

The next evening, Load Toad returns to The Skyline and finds a young woman in white-fringed go-go boots draped naked across his bed.

"You're a tall one, all right," says Load Toad. He scoops her clothing off the floor and throws it at her. When she is dressed, he marches her onto the lift. As they descend to the brothel on the fifth floor, she scales the walls and braces her feet on the handrails. Squatting above, she flashes her bare crotch at Load Toad then dismounts with a bounce.

"Christ, you're bendy," says Load Toad with some admiration.

She curtsies and exits the lift ahead of him.

The brothel is surprisingly bright, businesslike, underneath fluorescent lights that cast no shadows. As Load Toad hands the girl over to the front desk clerk, a gaggle of businessmen tumble out of the lift and Load Toad recognizes a glassware dealer from a trade show he attended in Shanghai the year prior.

"Happy," calls Load Toad. "What're you doing here?"

"Celebrating a contract signing," says Happy.

"Lucky bastard," says Load Toad. Stalled contract negotiations. School fees. His old man. Load Toad's forehead feels incredibly tight.

"You join us?" asks Happy, waving a pale hand at the reception desk clerk.

"No, no. You go ahead," says Load Toad.

"Chinese people are free," says Happy.

Load Toad doesn't know what to say.

"Chinese people are free," repeats Happy and adjusts his eyeglasses. "Free from Mao."

Alone in his hotel room, Load Toad drinks several glasses of rum and thinks about a country of brothels full of men celebrating Mao's death, thirty years after the fact.

Next door, The American arrives after midnight and turns on his television, louder than usual. Load Toad finds it impossible to sleep. At 2:00 AM Load Toad knocks on his door and asks him to turn it down. The American, wearing only his underpants, sways in the open doorway and says, "I'm celebrating four weeks at The Skyline."

He invites Load Toad in for a drink.

I'm stuck in a variety show worse than the one with the fucking clowns. Load Toad declines. The half-empty bottle of rum in his room is shouting.

I'll never last four weeks at The Line in the Sky, contract or no contract. Load Toad throws his belongings into his suitcase.

తతత

At night, Guangzhou is a haze of construction dust, a purple desert, through which skyscrapers emerge like robots. The taxi floats down empty streets. For some reason they're caught in a snarl of traffic in the side streets around the TV Tower site. *Why is every middle-of-the-night taxi ride like this?*

Electrical lines swing from bamboo pole to bamboo pole, feeding the temporary residences that crowd the entrance. Old people squat around charcoal fires, drinking tea, guarding their sleeping grandchildren. Somebody, somewhere is playing the national anthem.

On the rubble heap, scavengers with miners' headlamps clamber over the mound, search for scrap metal and wire, rush to extract what they can before the debris is trucked to the countryside and abandoned. There will always be someone squatting in the rubble of soviet bloc housing.

"Hurry, hurry," says Load Toad.

The taxi driver nods in the gloom of the front seat.

The taxi inches forward.

Three dogs stand at the top of the rubble heap and shout like outraged citizens. Like when the police arrive and drag you into the secret night. The faces of your neighbours turn silently away, leaving a trio of dogs to protest.

Eventually the taxi rounds the corner behind the TV Tower and the reason for the traffic jam is revealed. A night market has sprung up. In a roadside stall, a young woman turns and the flight of her hair travels through Load Toad back to his wife, asleep in their bed in Hong Kong, one arm draped across her beautiful face. He wonders if he could cry.

That's when a scavenger shoves through the plastic sheeting and offers to a grandmother a hand-made basket overflowing with scrap. She squats in the dust, untangles wires with fingers gnarled like ginger root. This is the memory that Load Toad will seek words for, when he watched an old woman pluck wire from a basket like a bird. He will repeat this story over and over, and search for meaning. In the end, he will wonder if he loves China.

The TV Tower watches over us all. Like a god, even though I don't believe in gods that abandon people to scavenge for scrap currency.

At the train station, Load Toad hears the sliced steel of an express train. He rattles the padlocked gate until a security guard approaches.

"21:23. Last train. 21:23," says the guard and points at the solitude of a train platform with his baton. A train sits there, under a spotlight, neither moving forward or backward. Eventually, the security guard provides Load Toad with a printed schedule for the train to Lo Wu and tells him to come back in the morning.

The same taxi driver lifts Load Toad's suitcase into the trunk of the same taxi.

When Load Toad returns to the same room at The Skyline Business Hotel, the Night Porter silently delivers a tray with tea and a fresh fruit basket. Hot jasmine tea and heavily-waxed cherry tomatoes tooth-picked into a pyramid.

The Dirty Duck

ON THE SECOND evening, the electricity goes out. Bill grabs a flashlight from a basket at the front desk and leaves. Past an elephant statue with hibiscus tucked in its folded hands, down the stone staircase and onto the terraced grounds of the Hotel Kebun Indah, he walks in search of something to eat.

The hotel is set back from the road and Bill follows an uneven pathway. A moon emerges, low on the horizon. The flashlight weakens as he walks alongside fields filled with rice sheaves, ready for harvest. Stone walls mark the boundaries. When the beam fades to nothing, he makes do with the green glow of his cellphone. It's difficult but, once his eyes adjust to the darkness, it's quite light. The soft skin of night is scratched with stars.

His cellphone buzzes.

"Bill? It's Mum. How're you going?"

"Great. Middle of the rice fields. What can I do for you?"

"Oh. I just called. How're you going?"

"Mum, you already asked me that. What's wrong?"

After a moment or two, she launches into a worry. "They used staples. They should've used stitches. What if it bursts?"

"What've you been doing? Bicycling into town? You're four weeks post-op, Mum. Take it easy." Bill fits his fingers into the mossy grooves of the stone wall. He changed Mum's dressing. An incision held together by a curved line of metal clips, stick insects.

"Looks good," he said. But when he plucked gauze squares from the dressing tray with plastic tweezers, he noticed his hands trembled slightly and couldn't make them stop.

"It's not infected, is it?" She hugged her nightgown closer to her body, peered over the accordion folds of peach-coloured fabric.

"It's clean," he said and applied adhesive strips for reinforcement. The midline incision was indicative of Wertheim's Procedure, a radical hysterectomy.

"I just shifted the patio furniture."

Mum. He wrenched his knee moving that teak furniture when he was in Melbourne last month, helping her. A strange trip. Dressing changes and patio furniture.

"No heavy lifting for another month," he says. Tries to keep impatience out of his voice and fails.

"How am I supposed to get things done?"

"You're just supposed to get better, Mum. That's all you're supposed to do."

"You're coming home next month for Dave's graduation, right?"

"Yes, Mum."

"Did I tell you? Maggie wants the whole family to get together for dinner to celebrate. Barbeque by the pool. You should see her new condo, Bill. Deluxe." Bill doesn't respond. Support payments are high and he resents money spent in ways he doesn't approve; Maggie shouldn't have sold the house.

"C'mon, Bill. It's one night. For Dave. You only graduate uni once, right?"

Bill reluctantly agrees. His relationship with Maggie is difficult. After nine years, he is surprised by her bitterness. The jibes about escaping to Asia. Christ, he married her, didn't he? He did the best he could. Dave's the one good thing that came out of their marriage.

Before Bill hangs up, he reminds Mum to call him immediately with her biopsy results, reassures her that otherwise, he'll telephone as soon as he arrives back in Hong Kong.

There's a rustling in the foliage. Bill startles, loses his balance on the uneven pathway and halts. Then there's jingling. What? A ring-nosed water buffalo sticks its face between the coconut palms and potted plants.

"Christ, are you trying to kill me?"

Pointy ears twitching, the water buffalo slowly swings its delicate head in his direction, as if to say no. They stare at one another for a moment, then the animal lowers its head to pull on shoots of elephant grass.

"A fucking water buffalo." Bill checks his pulse. It's running a bit high. Then there's his elevated blood pressure and intermittent chest pain to worry about, his doctor talking medication and serious lifestyle changes.

He stumbles onto pavement. The road is dark. The only light comes from passing cars and he pauses when a motorcycle brushes past. There's a pretty girl on the back and she's gripping the driver with her thighs, leaning back with her hands on the seat. Her skin is ochre against her T-shirt, blue-white in the sweeping headlights of oncoming traffic. When he closes his eyes, the shape of the girl flashes on the inside of his eyelids like a contrast x-ray. When was the last time he held a girl in his arms?

৯৯৯

Bell's Beach. A crowd of surfers sat around a bonfire each weekend and drank beer. That's where Bill met Maggie, on the beach, and they hit it off right away. Weeks passed in a blur of sex and surf. Their hurried sex, in the back of his car and on the beach, was fun. It was safer for him to think about it as fooling around but when he used the term at the bonfire one night, she grew angry and quit talking. Then she disappeared down the beach with his mate and he heard them laughing together. Propped against his surfboard, he stared at the night sky and waited for the blush of daybreak.

On Sunday afternoon, they sullenly drove back to Melbourne. Not far off the M1, a bush fire burned. The margin of the fire, a ragged line, scorched the grassland. The blue sky was clear of clouds and black smoke lifted from the ground in a raking rush.

Bill pulled over and parked, dug a camera out of his knapsack. He took several photos before he noticed Maggie standing next to him.

"What are you doing?" she asked.

"Documenting the end of this stupid fucking weekend."

"I didn't sleep with him."

"Why'd you go off with him, then?"

"You hurt my feelings, Bill. We aren't just fooling around. It's more than that, isn't it?"

"Christ, Maggie. I don't know what we're doing. Having fun?"

They stared helplessly at the fire. A helicopter, flying low and fast, dumped a water bomb, and the flames roared back. Sirens blared in the distance. When the wind picked up, a line of fire broke away, advancing across the grassland in a series of thrusts and parries. Its speed was astonishing; trees exploded on contact with flames. A kangaroo raced, erratic, frightened, across the road. When a series of police cars and fire trucks arrived, the uniformed men started setting up a roadblock.

"Let's get out of here," said Maggie. Together, they ran back to the car and drove away before traffic came to a complete standstill, the road clogged with firewatchers streaming out from the city. The Saints played on the radio, a song about being stranded far from home.

Maggie sat close, her small hand rested lightly on his thigh. He kept his eyes on the road, not daring to acknowledge her touch, afraid of interrupting the intimacy. It took a while to reach her parents' and, by the time they pulled into their drive, the confusion of the weekend dissipated.

And they continued having fun for a little while longer. Until she told him about the pregnancy and he knew that he had paddled out too far, that he was in dangerous waters. Untethered from his surfboard. Under pressure from his mum, he did what was expected. Dave was born five months after the wedding.

ॐॐॐ

Without warning, he's ankle deep in a flooded rice field and strangely he isn't worried about how he arrived here, nor the possibility of water and mosquito-borne illness. Instead, he removes his sandals and squishes his toes in the muck, enjoying the sensation until tough roots press too deeply into his soles.

Splashing. What? Bill uses his cellphone light and peers into the dark. A man wearing a black-and-white sarong stomps up and silently points at the ornate, wooden headdress he wears. The top of the headdress is a tall, triangular-shaped crown with a line of five little heads sticking out either side. The man removes it and offers it to Bill.

"You want me to wear it?"

The man nods, his smooth, young face glows green.

Bill takes the headdress and carefully places it on his own head. It's heavy and cuts into his neck. The man roars fiercely in his face. Bill strikes a diabolical pose with his elbows and knees bent, and roars back. The crown wobbles. The man is laughing, shoulders heaving. Then he turns and stomps into the shadows of the rice field. At one point, he stops to wave.

"Don't you want it back?" Bill shouts and points.

The man disappears behind a stone shed that tilts at an angle, a trick of moonlight slanting through the trees. There's a gust of wind and silver-tipped plants whip against one another, each edge separate and distinct. Bill reaches out and touches. Sharp, smooth.

A random left turn. Another road. He pats his head and face, feeling for the crown. Shifts it to a more comfortable position. Sandals in hand, Bill walks, the rough road beneath his feet. The road is unmarked. It doesn't matter. Sooner or later, it will turn onto another road and when it does it will cross a river that is slow and quiet and hidden; and, on the other side, a string of roadside restaurants and bars.

In the distance the sky is glowing. He rounds a corner, and then another. There it is. The Dirty Duck. It's shining against the night sky, light streaming through the open walls, burning in the dark. Two stories high, it looms over the rice fields that surround it. It is so bright it seems to lean back, like the sky is holding it up. A hostess beckons. Bill steps across the threshold.

The restaurant is full and the hostess settles him into a seat at the bar.

"What would the king like to drink?" asks the bartender. His hair is combed carefully to one side and he moves discreetly.

Scanning the drink menu, Bill focuses on the house special noted as "The Best Martini in Ubud". He orders a double and, when it arrives, asks, "Is there vodka in it?"

"Yes."

"Is a vodka martini, strictly speaking, a martini?"

The bartender nods.

"Having read Frank Moorhouse's book on the subject, I would have to respectfully disagree. This is a vodkatini. Cheers." Icy cold slides down his throat.

"You have many responsibilities as king."

"God, no. I don't have any responsibilities. I'm here for a medical conference."

A little later the bartender says, "You like to read. Me, also. My name is Made. Now we are more friends."

Bill introduces himself.

In between drink orders, Bill and Made discuss Nordic mysteries. "*The Laughing Policeman* is my favourite," says Bill and orders a double vodkatini. It occurs to him that he isn't feeling any effects from the liquor.

A girl with blonde dreadlocks settles into a stool down the bar and talks quietly with Made. When she catches Bill's eye she says, "I'll have what the king's having," and points at his drink.

"It's a vodkatini," says Bill. He leans forward and loud-whispers, "Be forewarned."

"No worries, no worries." She slips her bead-laden hair over her shoulder. The ends clatter together like seashells and, for some reason, Bill wonders if she surfs.

"The best martini in Ubud. Says so on the drinks menu."

"How is it?"

"It's a fucking fine drink. But I wouldn't call it a martini."

The girl asks Made how business is and he shrugs and says, "You finish work, Carolyn?"

She nods and says, "God, I need a drink." When she winds her ankles around the legs of her stool, her flip-flops drop to the tiled floor. Her feet are tanned, striped white skin where straps used to be. Her toes are calloused and dirty.

"Rough day?" asks Bill.

"Endless cakes." She moves her hand in the air like she's knocking aside a stack of tins. Her hands are thin like her face but beneath her suntan she is pale.

Made explains she's a baker at Café Wayan and describes her chocolate cake in detail, a favourite with locals and visitors alike. He ends by saying, "American style. Very good to you."

"Backpackers love it," says Carolyn and shrugs. "Reminds them of home, I guess."

"You should be careful with flour dust. Clogs your lungs. You don't want to end up with an occupational illness."

"You're a doctor?" Her eyes widen for a moment. They're brown with gold flecks around her pupils. Brown eyes remind him of Maggie.

"Radiologist, although I've let my licence lapse. I sell radiology equipment." Bill hands his name card down the bar. "You ever need an x-ray, give me a call and I'll point you in the direction of a hospital with the latest technology."

"Thanks, I'll keep that in mind." Carolyn stands and slides the paper rectangle into the back pocket of her cut-offs. Her shorts hang off slim hips and there's a small tattoo above where her kite-shaped uterus is located, folded slightly forward.

Mum waved goodbye, standing, crooked, in the front doorway of her house, holding a pillow to her abdomen. She tried not to grimace. And it occurs to him that Mum could die, that it would fall to him to clear up her unfinished business.

"Did you decide how to advertise the taxi?" Carolyn asks Made.

"Yes. I use Twitter," says Made.

"How's it going?"

"I think I can sell to my plan."

"Driving taxi and bartending. You work hard," says Bill.

Made nods. "Yes. I have two jobs. Bali is not anymore what it used to be. I am forced to get out from the land."

"The government expropriated a chunk of farm land, including Made's family compound, and handed it over to hotel developers," explains Carolyn.

"Jakarta government, not Balinese government," says Made. His expression is serious.

"I'm sorry to hear that," says Bill.

Made carefully wipes down the counter before he says, "Bali is change. Many places in Indonesia have no change." Then he carries a rack of dirty glasses to the kitchen. Cleaning up paradise.

"Your feet are covered in mud, Bill."

"Took a shortcut through the rice fields," says Bill. Muck and roots pressed into his bared feet. He cannot understand how he found himself first on one road, then another.

"Did you get lost?"

"Little bit. There was a man. In the rice field. The second rice field. He gave me the crown. My mum was in the first rice field. On the phone. Christ, I sound like a nutter."

Carolyn nods. "Bali's a weird place."

"What are you doing here?"

"Having fun," says Carolyn. "I'm young. That's what you do when you're young, isn't it?"

"Sometimes you have to grow up. I got married. And divorced." Bill stares at his crowned reflection in the bar mirror; it looks like the heads are multiplying exponentially.

"Which is exactly why I'm travelling. I'll go back to The States next year. I've been thinking about graduate school at Berkeley. I don't know. In the meantime, I bake."

"Is the cake good?"

"It's totally fantastic. And I'm not just saying that because I made it."

"Secret ingredient?"

Carolyn nods and sips her vodkatini.

"What is it?"

"Love," says Carolyn simply. "You want some?"

"Cake?"

Carolyn nods and finishes her drink in one gulp. "Let's go."

On their way out, Carolyn says, "Wait." She squats and scoops a small frog stranded on the walkway. Cradling it in cupped hands, she walks to the edge of a water garden and releases it onto a lily pad.

వావావా

At the Café Wayan, Carolyn pulls a multi-layered chocolate cake from the takeout cooler by the front entrance, and slices a generous wedge into a Styrofoam container. Bill and Carolyn stand in the narrow road next to a clutter of parked motorcycles.

A large group of men wearing black-and-white sarongs and sneakers with fluorescent stripes, carrying backpacks slung casually over their shoulders, stream across the road and momentarily block traffic. As they brush past, several of them are texting or listening to music on earphones.

"Who are those guys?"

"Traditional Balinese dancers."

Glancing back, Bill shifts the crown and rubs the back of his head. Balinese people. One foot in the rice field, one foot in the digital world.

"Well?" she asks after he forks down the slice.

"It's fucking fantastic. The best chocolate cake I've ever had."

"It was my mother's recipe," says Carolyn.

"Was?"

"She died a couple of years ago. Pancreatic cancer. It was a horrible death, Bill. Horrible."

"Cancer's a right bastard. My Mum just had a hysterectomy for a large cancerous mass. No treatment plans yet, although the staging is due any day."

"Will you go home?"

"Yes," he says without thinking, and realizes that his life as an expat is coming to an end. It's not much of a life. Seldom home, he sees his friends once a month, usually at The Globe. And as a silent partner in the busy pub, his input isn't required for the day-to-day operations, just his money. He is going home.

"I'm sorry, Bill." Carolyn reaches across and hugs him. The crown slips. He pats her back awkwardly. Her scent is a mixture of sweat, patchouli, and ginger. On impulse, he touches her dreadlocks and they feel like tatted wool. It occurs to him that Carolyn is probably the same age as Dave and that he has no business touching her hair.

"I see you, Bill."

"What do you see?"

"All kinds of stuff."

"My sternum is aching."

"It's understandable, totally understandable."

"It's angina, actually. I thought it was a heart attack the first time it happened but it's angina."

She smacks him. "I was talking about your mum. And you touched my hair, you perv."

"You're woolly," says Bill.

"I know," says Carolyn and pulls him closer, still.

Forcing himself to relax, Bill settles into the embrace. It feels good to be in a girl's arms again. One summer, in what seems like another life, he partied on Bell's Beach with the surfers, having fun. Later that summer, he sat with a girl on the edge of a bonfire. There was an image of her imprinted in his memory. Sitting cross-legged on a blanket, she turned toward him, her hair tousled from the breeze, her face open and smiling. Her bared feet were covered with a fine layer of sand.

Bill realizes that he never really committed. That he turned away from her from the start. When he sees her at Dave's graduation, he could say something. Anything. He could do that much. What he means is that he could do that much for her, for that girl on the beach.

ক্ষ ক্ষ ক্ষ

The next morning, Bill lies beneath a cool, cotton sheet at the Hotel Kebun Indah and checks his phone for a message about a biopsy. Nothing. His crown is on the floor beside his muddy sandals. His scalp is tender where he palpates a slight bump on his occipital bone. He listens to roosters crowing in the distance, thinking that he once was a good surfer, thinking that he is no longer young. Thinking it doesn't matter anymore. He is alone. There was this girl, in another life, Maggie, and there was another girl, in this life, Carolyn. That is all. Carolyn, with dreadlocks and dirty tanned feet. Holding him on a dark night in Ubud.

Drinks List

Heineken
mojito
JD
Beamish
Coca-Cola
scotch-scotch
whiskey
gin tonic
duty-free Bacardi
vodkatini

Playlist

"Head Above Water "by Hunters & Collectors
"Disorder" by Joy Division
"This is not a love song" by PIL
"Temptation" by New Order
"Pacific Theme" by Broken Social Scene
"The Fairytale of New York" by The Pogues (with Kirsty McColl)
"Ever Fallen in Love" by The Buzzcocks
"Ceremony" by New Order
"Stranded" by The Saints
"Stars & Sons" by Broken Social Scene
"Forget Myself" by Elbow
"Love Will Tear Us Apart" by Joy Division

Notes & Acknowledgements

Earlier versions of several of these stories appeared in the following publications:

"Rephrasing Kate" *The New Quarterly*

"Leon" *The Fiddlehead*

"The Suitable Dress" *Grain*

Thank you to the editors of each. Your support meant everything to this isolated writer.

I gratefully acknowledge the support of the Banff Centre, the Alberta Foundation for the Arts, and the Calgary Foundation. Also, I thank the Humber School for Writers and, in particular, Trevor Cole for expert counsel on the manuscript.

A special thank you to my friend and writing partner Beth Everest, who provided essential feedback over the years. Thank you to fellow writing colleagues for their manuscript reviews on selected stories: Jeramy Dodds, Charlotte Gill, Lori Hahnel, Lee Kvern, Melanie Little, and Deborah Willis.

I owe a debt of gratitude to Andrew Mountford and the gang at HK Expats for the fun and inspiration.

Finally, thanks to Al Forrie, Jackie Forrie, editor Seán Virgo, and the rest of the crew at Thistledown Press. Your insight into and enthusiasm for this collection of stories are much appreciated.